RUDY'S *Heart*

LAURIE RYAN

www.laurieryanauthor.com

DEDICATION

To those who love horses,
a feeling I hope
never goes away.

CHAPTER ONE

Tail flying high, the horse raced to the far end of the corral and reared when the fence prevented his escape. He whirled around, kicking at fence boards that bounced with the force of the blow but withstood the battering. Once, twice, three times he kicked. When he finally dropped to four legs, he stood there shivering, his coat glossy with sweat.

Beck Hawthorne settled a booted foot on the lowest board and leaned on the fence, wondering for the thousandth time in the last month why he'd taken on this horse. Brought to Beck from an abusive situation, Rudy wouldn't let a soul near him. He'd bitten two of Beck's men and tried to kick a third when they'd moved him from the trailer to this corral. When they'd tried to bathe him, he'd fought until they were forced to stop or risk injury, to the horse or to them. Rudy had been so terrified, Beck couldn't put him through that again. Now, Beck wouldn't let any of his men near the horse. He alone set out food and mucked out the lean-to at the end of the corral, the one they'd built so Rudy would have more shade and a place to eat. Not that he'd gotten any thanks for it. Nope. Nothing but angry puffs of air from the far side of the corral whenever he entered with food or pitchfork. Rudy ate the feed, but only after Beck retreated from sight.

How could he get through to this animal? Everything he'd tried so far had dismal results. And now his young niece seemed taken with the horse. Damn it. Beck slapped the fence and the horse jumped even with the distance between them. He yanked his hat off and wiped sweat from his brow with his arm.

"Beck?"

Cassidy, the face of Hope Ranch and Beck's go-to for all things organizational, stood several feet back, toying with a strand of kinky hair that had four or five colors woven through it, colors that complemented her dark skin. She eyed the horse as she held out a phone. "Mara's asking for you and won't take no for an answer."

Mara. His favorite cousin, even if she was a royal pain in the ass. Okay, his only cousin. With a last glance at the horse, Beck thanked Cassidy and took the phone.

"Hey, Mars."

"Yeah, and that nickname never gets old," she drawled. "How's my favorite little girl doing?"

Dani. The niece he'd been given sole custody of. The worry knot in Beck's throat tightened. "She's no better, no worse. She's healthy, fed, seems content. I just can't get her to open up, to tell me how to help her."

"Give it time," Mara said. "It hasn't been that long."

"It's been months."

"Not very many, though. Grief takes its own time. She'll let you know when she's ready to talk. In the meantime, just love her and let her enjoy the ranch. By the way, where the heck were you hiding? I could have painted my nails and dried them in the time it took your assistant to find you."

"I live on a ranch now, remember? Nothing's a short walk. You know that." He nodded to Cassidy, thinking that would act as a dismissal, but she stayed where she was. Beck should have known better. His ranch manager's daughter kept this place running smoothly, though her attitude got a bit proprietary at times.

"Yes, dear cousin, I do," Mara said. "Speaking of which, how's everything going?"

Beck headed back toward the house. When Cassidy fell in step beside him, he glared at her, but he knew she wouldn't budge. If she wasn't so good at her job ...

"Things are slow," he told Mara. She had a right to know. She'd been there to help for the first couple weeks after he'd bought the place. "The barn is ready and I'm searching for the right quarter horses to begin the breeding program. Since it could take years for that to be profitable, I hope to bring in several hundred head of cattle this fall, which means we're working on fencing."

"And the house?"

"The bed and breakfast is a low priority, but it's coming along."

"Good, because I've got your first customer, a woman I know."

"Mars, we're not open yet." The B&B idea had been Cassidy's. Beck had thought her nuts, but anything that would make some money for the pit into which he'd sunk a huge chunk of his finances couldn't be a bad idea, right? Now, he was back to thinking it was crazy.

"It will be a good run-through for the guest part of your ranch. And she'll be no trouble. She just needs a place to rest for a while."

Rest? How old was this woman? "Absolutely not. I don't even have the rooms furnished yet. The furniture doesn't arrive for another two weeks."

"Then move a bed, dresser, and chair from the bunkhouse to that room at the front. It's the quietest and has the best view."

Instantly, Beck regretted Mara's visit to the ranch after his niece came to live with him. She'd been a huge help, but the woman remembered too much.

"Come on, Beckett. She needs a break and you need a test guest. It's a win-win."

The sting of hearing that name punched Beck in the gut. He hadn't gone by that in years. Since college, to be exact. Since his father, Beckett, Sr., had died, along with Beck's mother. Beckett brought back too many memories, some of which were tied to fresh wounds.

"We could bring furniture up, but— "

"Good, because her name is Aubrey Gannet and she's already on her way."

"What?"

"Yep. I saw her off this morning. Figured you'd come around and recognize the benefit for both of you. She's driving from Seattle and isn't a speedy traveler, so it'll be three days before she arrives. She won't stay long. I promise. Just a few days."

Great. Some old woman who drove fifty miles per hour on the freeway. Beck pictured her on Montana's highways, a line of traffic honking behind her. "That's not enough time," he told Mara.

"Sure it is. But Becky?"

And there it was. The other name he preferred to never hear again. He hated that childhood name, gifted to him by the one and only Mara. If she weren't the one person he could count on, he'd give her an earful.

"Take it easy on her, okay? She's had it rough and really needs to rest."

"Who are you sending me? Someone who's sick or something?"

"Not sick. Tired."

Great. Not only a guest he wasn't ready for, but a guest with issues. Beck glanced back at Rudy, who'd moved to his fresh food. In the opposite direction, Dani stared through a window, another lost soul, her eyes riveted on that damn horse. The look of longing on her face was something Beck didn't need words to decipher. Grief had turned his six-year-old niece into a silent ball of sadness. She seemed lonely, too, though she was rarely alone. Now, some old lady who'd probably need more help than Mara thought was on her way to join them. From Seattle. Where Dani had lived until coming to live with him.

Somehow, he'd become a home for wounded souls. Beck clicked off the call with Mara and handed the phone to Cassidy, who'd kept pace with him.

"It seems we're about to have company. Have someone bring up the best bed and dresser from the bunkhouse and put it in the front bedroom upstairs."

"Who's coming?"

"I have no idea. Mara sent her. Some lady who needs to rest. Apparently, we've turned into a recovery home for the aged. And the young. And horses."

~~~

"What have you gotten me into?" Aubrey Gannet muttered, and not for the first time, to the woman listening on the other end of the phone, the culprit behind her predicament.

"This will be good for you," Mara said. "You need to get away for a while."
~~~

"I need to relax, not disappear. I just left Butte, and it already seems like I'm in the middle of nowhere." She'd left her comfort zone way behind. It had been a while since she'd traveled anywhere except to visit patients, and now, she was two states away from home and lost. It had taken her until well past noon to find the motivation to get going, which left zero time to un-lose herself. "Plus, didn't you say it would be temperate this time of year?"

A sheen of sweat covered the tops of her hands and her palms stuck to the steering wheel. Aubrey peeled them off and wiped them, one at a time, on her jeans. Sweat was her nervous release, though it generally made matters worse rather than better. Still, today was sweltering. Her old car overheated without much convincing. Not wanting to break down on the far side of nowhere, she'd opted for windows-down air conditioning, though that resulted in the scent of sun-baked everything permeating the air inside her car.

"If there's nothing around you, you must be close, which means you're going to lose cell service soon."

"Lose cell service?" Oh, this was so going from bad to worse.

"Yes ... remember ... relax and don't ... anyone ask you ... help. Tell ... him ... be nice. Goodb— "

With that unfinished word, Aubrey's cell cut out, apparently for the duration of her visit to Nowhere, Montana.

Running a hand along her neck, Aubrey yanked her ponytail, a miserable failure at keeping her cooler, over her shoulder. She sighed. How had Mara talked her into this? A week ago, she'd shown up at Aubrey's apartment with a bottle of wine. By the end of that bottle, she'd elicited a promise from Aubrey—a mandatory vacation—and had held her to it. Her friend had taken total advantage of her moment of weakness.

Aubrey needed a break. She knew that. Too much death had visited her of late. Normally, she handled that a lot better. As a hospice social worker, she considered it an extraordinary privilege to help patients cross that final threshold in as peace-filled a way as possible. That never used to get to her. Hope's passing had broken her, though. Work, life, everything – it all seemed so futile.

Hope Jones, the dark-haired, thirty-one-year-old with brown, soulful eyes, had handled her cancer with quiet calmness, her entire focus on her young daughter. Seeing that relationship, Aubrey had longed for her own family, her own children.

Then Hope died and the little girl drew into herself. Nothing Aubrey did brought the girl out of her shell. She'd tried over several days to help the silent sadness in the six-year-old's face, to no avail. Aubrey had considered trying to fast-track a foster-parent application.

That's when the child had disappeared. Whisked away by some relative Hope had only mentioned once, and even then, she'd barely said anything. A brother. He'd never come to visit Hope in the months Aubrey had been part of her life. And Hope's no-account ex-husband had disappeared before the positive symbol on the pregnancy test had become clear. Hope had confided in Aubrey that the man had sent papers giving up all his rights to his daughter in the same envelope as the divorce papers.

Had Hope asked her no-account brother to take the child? Aubrey had a hard time believing she would do that. Aubrey had tried to find the six-year-old. No matter how much Aubrey begged child services, no one would tell her where the brother lived. Even Mara, the girl's cousin, had been close-mouthed, giving Aubrey some cockamamie story that she needed to heal herself first.

After that, her job became more burden than blessing. She'd tried to give her patients the best care, to hide her tears for the families and friends. She'd buried her own emotions pretty well, she'd thought. Until her boss put her on a mandatory leave of absence.

"Get your head back in the game and your heart out of it." Gwen said the words with gentle effect, and then reminded Aubrey how good she was at hospice work and that they'd hate to lose her.

"Burnout is real," Gwen said.

So, after two weeks of Aubrey barely sleeping and eating, Mara had shown up at her door.

Aubrey glared at the semi-arid, empty landscape passing by her car window. Friend or no friend, when she got home, she would pound Mara.

After another mile, fenced fields appeared on both sides of the road. Then, finally, the typical tall wooden and metal structure that heralded the entrance to a ranch. Aubrey turned off the road and stopped. A mailbox had the name Hawthorne on it. That's the name Mara had given her. Her gaze moved up to the sign swaying in the welcome breeze.

Hope Ranch.

Aubrey's heart pounded, her hand the only thing keeping it from thumping right out of her chest. The name brought all the pain and grief, never far from her mind, roaring to the forefront. She looked at the address Mara gave her. The same numbers were screwed to the fence post in front of her. This was the right place.

Had Mara known? Aubrey swiped at the tears that fell unbidden. Hope. Too young to have her life snuffed out. The pain was real. Her gut spasmed as she thought of the last moments in her friend's life. And now the grief surged, being here, at a place with her friend's name on the front gate. She got out of the car and walked to the fence, looking each way at the long stretch of board and post that followed the road until she couldn't see it anymore. Her hand hovered over the wood for a long moment before resting on its roughness.

Hope.

I miss you so much.

How had Mara found this place? Sent her here? Aubrey couldn't do this. Couldn't stay where everything would be wrapped around memories of her lost friend. She got in her car, resolute about turning around, heading back to Butte. Grabbing the steering wheel, she leaned forward and rested her forehead on her hands.

It hurt so much. Everything hurt. How was she ever going to be happy again?

She gazed up at the stylized sign, remembering how Hope had whiled away hours with pen and paper in her hand, doodling those same types of curly-cues. She'd gifted Aubrey with one of her pages of doodles. Tesla would have been proud of the freehand designs. And she treasured the gift, which lay framed and safely tucked in her suitcase.

If she turned around and went home, she'd have to listen to Mara's consternation for days or weeks on end. Maybe she should spend a night, check it out. Then, Mara would get off her case and she could get back to the rightful depression she'd been mired in.

The sun was well on its way down the westward path to setting, so she might not make it back to Butte by nightfall. Driving solo on a pitch-black, lonely road wasn't a smart choice. So be it. Aubrey straightened. One night. Anything could be tolerated for one night, right? She started the engine and, since she only had a short way to go, she put the windows up and turned on the blessed air conditioning.

As she headed down the winding driveway, she followed fencing that separated pastures into a perfect, idyllic setting, just like in the movies. This ranch used blond wood fencing that seemed to melt into the view, not stand out. It looked right. On one side, several horses stood, enjoying the late afternoon heat. One neighed, making Aubrey smile as she remembered riding all those years ago. She'd planned to have her own horses by twenty, but life had taken her in a more urban direction. Living in Seattle had left no room for equestrian hobbies. As she neared the ranch house, Aubrey noticed a lone horse in a fenced area on the other side. Aubrey squinted to get a better view in the sunshine. A brown and white, very dirty horse watched her with troubled, soulful eyes while she drove past.

She parked in front of a two-story, sprawling house. Having never been on a ranch before, Aubrey only had movies to guide her perception. This didn't stray far from those ideals. With a wrap-around porch and siding that looked like reclaimed barn wood, it didn't look old. Rather, it looked homey, with brushes of color in standing and hanging flower pots. Chairs, gliders, and small tables dotted the porch and an American flag hung from a small post jutting out above white-washed stairs that invited you to enter.

Stepping out of the car, Aubrey took a deep breath. At that moment, as she gazed around, peace filled her to the point she didn't want to move. To stay here, to feel a tranquility foreign to her these days, was a blessing. Aubrey closed her eyes and turned her face to the sun, accepting the heat as part of what made this moment feel good.

She couldn't stand there forever, though, so she popped the trunk and pulled out her suitcase, closing it quietly. She didn't want to disturb the serenity. Before she headed inside to locate someone, she looked back at the lone horse. He stood on the far side of the pasture and she could see him shivering. She set her suitcase down, her feet drawn toward the fence, her eyes focused on the horse. Something had hurt him. She could sense the pain, feel the fear.

The horse held her gaze as she reached for the wood fence slat. She stood there, silent and still, waiting. It took a while, but the horse stepped in her direction, moving toward her like one of those slow-motion commercials with Clydesdales. Except this was no workhorse. This boy was sleek and dappled in the white and brown striations of a pinto. Aubrey couldn't remember anything or anyone looking as handsome as this guy, even though the matting and mud-caking of his hair had turned the white patches to a dull gray.

The strangest sensation filled her as the horse got closer, as if she was coming home. When the horse stopped in front of her, Aubrey reached out her hand.

"Stop!"

CHAPTER TWO

Beck turned away just for a moment. That was all. He'd been watching the horse from his office, saw the car drive in and park. This had to be Mara's friend. Then he got distracted by a text from his foreman. Seconds, really. When he'd glanced back, the woman had her hand outstretched like she planned to actually touch that damn horse.

He yanked open his office window. "Stop!" He held his breath until she paused and looked his way, then he slammed the window shut, raced through the house and wrenched the door open. Beck launched himself off the porch, landing hard on the ground. He broke into a run, fueled by fear-laced adrenaline. He had to get to the woman, keep Rudy from biting her.

He reached out, grabbed the woman's still outstretched arm, and snatched her back and away from the horse. Rudy reared, pawing the air so close to them that he almost came down on the fence boards. Beck put distance between them and the horse as Rudy tossed his head, huffed, twisted around, and kicked out again, this time with his back feet. The wood shook with the force of the hit. Rudy took off, not stopping until he reached the far side of the corral, his chest hitting the fence with a resounding thunk.

"What the hell were you thinking?" he asked the woman, loosening his hold now that the danger had passed. He turned to her, ready to read her the riot act, only to have the earth yanked out from beneath him. Everything hit him at once: her night-sky-blue eyes, the fact she wasn't an old crone by any definition, her fist connecting with his jaw.

His head whipped back. "What the hell?"

The stars circling his head cleared enough for him to see her bolt for her car.

"Hold up," he called. He followed her, still trying to de-cobweb his head as he ground his jaw back and forth. The woman packed a decent punch.

She turned on him as he neared, yanked her hand out of her purse. "Don't come any closer," she yelled, pointing something at his chest.

Beck squinted, his eyesight still a touch blurry. "What is that? A Taser?"

"Yes, and I'll use it." She dug back into her purse one-handed, coming up with a cell. "Don't move a muscle." She tapped her phone. "Damn." After a glance to each side, she centered her gaze on him again.

She looked ready to pull that damn trigger. If he didn't diffuse this situation and fast, more than just his jaw would get hurt. He held his hands up. "I won't hurt you." He pasted a smile on his face, having been told it was one of his best qualities and he should use it more.

"You already have."

That wiped the smile off. Had he grabbed her too hard? God, he hadn't meant to do that. Beck let the regret show on his face and in his voice. "I'm sorry. I truly am. But that horse is an angry mess. Bit two of my guys last week. If he'd gotten hold of you, well, I refused to let that happen."

The woman stared at him. When the fierceness left those amazing blue eyes, Beck knew she believed him.

She lowered the Taser, but Beck didn't lower his arms until she'd put it back in her purse and tossed her purse into the car. He let out a breath, slow and easy, the adrenaline siphoning off as he got a second look at the woman standing in front of him. Eyes like iced sapphires, framed by dark lashes and perfectly arched eyebrows. Her lower lip was full and he wanted to run his finger along it, her chin perfect for tipping up to meet his lips.

And the rest of her? His gaze ranged over her, seeing curves in all the right places. The right curves, athletic where they needed to be and enticing everywhere else. This was not the old woman he'd pictured based on Mara's comments.

"He wouldn't have hurt me."

"Who?" Still caught up in the vision in front of him, Beck didn't, at first, get what she said.

"The horse."

"Rudy? Oh, yes, he definitely would have."

She shook her head, that pouty lower lip now a grim line.

Beck's nostrils flared in irritation. "It doesn't matter what you think. This is my ranch, so you'll do what I say while you're on it. And I say stay away from that horse."

"You need some help, boss?" Cassidy spoke from the porch.

The woman whipped around at the new voice.

"Yes," he ground out. "This is Mara's friend, I'm assuming?" He cocked his head and glared at the woman until she nodded.

"Great. Show her the room. Let her know about dinner." He strode off, stopping after a few steps to look at her one more time. "Stay away from that horse or you'll be gone before you can unpack."

With that, he tore off at the quickest pace possible without the appearance of running away. That woman was trouble with a capital "T." The defiance clear in her face meant he'd need to keep a close eye on her. Didn't she know anything about horses? She might have been injured. Badly. He pictured himself picking her up, carrying her into the house, tending her wounds. Gah! Beck didn't need this. She was a distraction. A beautiful one, but a distraction he refused to tolerate right now. He should send her packing. In fact, Beck decided to tell her that first thing in the morning.

He was in the barn mucking out stalls when it hit him. For a woman Mara had described as frail, she had a lot of moxy.

~~~

"I'm Cassidy." The ebony-skinned woman with the wild-colored hair stepped off the porch and held her hand out to Aubrey, who shook it with some trepidation.

"Sorry, um, for the rude entrance. The boss gets a little crazy over that horse." She looked over Aubrey's shoulder and shuddered.

"You don't like horses?"

"No." Cassidy laughed. "It's crazy that I live on a horse ranch, isn't it?"

Her easy, genuine smile won Aubrey over. She smiled back. "It kind of is. By the way, I'm Aubrey."

"It's nice to meet you." Cassidy tipped an imaginary
~~~

hat. Not that any hat could sit atop that stack of hair. "My Dad's the manager here. We've moved a bit, from ranch to ranch. It's pretty much the only life I've ever known."

"Surrounded by animals you don't like?"

"Well, there's more to like than not. It's a good living," Cassidy said. "So, how about we get you settled?"

Aubrey shook her head. "I don't think I should stay."

"You can't leave before dinner. The food here is the best ever. Besides, driving at night isn't advisable. Lots of open space and no one around if you get into any trouble. At least stay until morning."

"I—I don't know." Aubrey glanced toward where the man had stalked off. Her nerves still jittered from when he'd yanked her right into his lean, hard body. Not just that, though. When those dark, serious eyes had checked her out, she'd tingled. He'd done the whole up and down thing, then scowled. Aubrey wasn't in any mood to be ogled, but that stung.

"Come on," Cassidy said. "Beck's all bark and no bite. Besides, you probably won't even see him." She leaned in. "He can get pretty reclusive. Stay the night. Rest. You can decide in the morning."

That seemed the safest option since dusk would fade to full night before she got back to Butte. She nodded.

"Great. I'll carry your suitcase. Just leave your car here. We can park it better once you decide to stay."

Aubrey grabbed her purse, closed and locked the door, and followed Cassidy into the house, still not sure this was the right decision.

"This is the formal living room. Down that way,"— Cassidy pointed down a long hallway with her free hand— "is the kitchen. Dinner's at seven sharp, so you'll have a little time to rest." She trudged up the stairs as if carrying Aubrey's suitcase was nothing.

At the top, she opened a door into a bedroom.

"This is the best view in the house."

She set Aubrey's suitcase on a bed covered in a checkerboard quilt. The room was large, though more bare than comfortable. Only a bed, chair, and dresser occupied it. No nightstand, no pictures on the wall, not even a hook for a bathrobe.

"I'm sorry there's not much here. The stuff for our guest rooms hasn't arrived yet. We brought these things up from the bunkhouse. But the bed's comfortable. The mattress is new. And this comforter, well, it'll keep you as warm as you want it to. I know, because it's mine. My mom made it."

"I don't want to take your blanket, Cassidy. I can make do with anything."

"Oh, it's fine. I don't use it, anyhow." Cassidy touched Aubrey's arm. "There's something special about you. I can sense things, and that's the vibe I get from you. Except ... " Cassidy cocked her head. "It's buried somehow, under a world of hurt, I'm guessing."

That was a lot of wisdom for such a young woman. And it cut too close to the heart of Aubrey's pain.

"I'm sorry," Cassidy said, giving her a hug. "I talk too much and say things I shouldn't, so I'll leave you to unpack. But I do get these feelings. And you being here, it's a good thing. For everyone. I understand if you choose to leave, but I hope you stay." There was a depth in her dark eyes that spoke to Aubrey.

"I promise I won't decide anything until morning."

"Great! See you for dinner!"

With that, she skipped out of the room, closing the door behind her.

Aubrey walked to the bed, running her hand along the quilt. It was a beautiful mish-mash of materials, all in small, intricate, vibrant-colored squares. She picked up an end. Handsewn. This must have taken hours and hours to complete. Gratitude at the loaned gift swelled in Aubrey's heart, easing her pain for a moment.

And her anger.

The one window in the room looked out on the driveway and pasture. At least it had curtains. Aubrey fingered the aging checkered material as she watched the horse pace. A horse with a lot of issues. Aubrey hadn't been near a horse in years, but her sixth sense, like Cassidy's, said he would never hurt her. Rudy. That name fit him. The pull to go back out there, to spend more time with him, surprised Aubrey.

Fat chance of that happening. Her ire with the ranch owner returned as she rubbed her arm. She'd be sore tomorrow. He'd grabbed her hard, and he'd had no right. Everything had been fine, Rudy content and gentle, until he mucked it all up. Things hadn't turned ugly until Beck had raced in to *save* her.

With that intense gaze, she figured nothing got past him. She'd had trouble seeing his eyes clearly under the hat, but they appeared as dark as his attitude. If she stayed, she'd have to keep well away from him. He was too present. Too handsome. And too much ... man. She didn't need that kind of complication right now, and she'd walked away from taking orders a long time ago.

Picking up her suitcase, Aubrey set it on the chair, unwilling to settle in by unpacking. She wasn't staying past breakfast anyhow, so instead, she sank onto the mattress, surprised at how comfortable it was. More so than her bed at home, a hand-me-down from Mara.

Hmm. Mara. Her friend had some explaining to do. Aubrey glanced at her phone. Still no bars.

Great.

Maybe there was a landline here so she could call Mara and explain how brilliant this idea of hers had been. How Mara had thought it would be good for Aubrey here, in this depressing place, remained a mystery. The owner was angry, and Rudy was in obvious pain. All the negative emotions swirled around her, dragging her down, wearing through her paper-thin defenses.

Aubrey lay on the bed and tugged the comforter over her, weary of everything. Thoughts of Hope came unbidden and always with a punch to her heart. Hope, with her genuine smile and caring demeanor. Hope, with her daughter on the bed, making doodles on paper. Hope, wasting away to nothing as the cancer destroyed her, yet still finding happiness in her day.

How would Aubrey ever return to her job? It hurt so much. All of it. She clutched the blanket to her like it would quiet the agitation in her gut. Her tears dampened the pillow and she closed her eyes tight, trying to stop the memories and emotions that flooded through her.

When she woke, full dark had descended and she found nothing familiar. Even the air smelled different. Hay and horses, that's what it was. She was at the ranch Mara had sent her to. The ranch run by that irritating man, Beck.

Sitting up, she reached for a bedside lamp before she remembered there wasn't one. Aubrey fumbled her way across to the window to look out over the ranch. The few lights did little to dispel the absolute darkness that surrounded the place, so different from the city lights she'd always known. This seemed so foreign to her.

She strained to see, looking for Rudy, but couldn't spot him in the shadows. Aubrey pulled the curtains closed against the darkness and switched on the overhead light, blinking at the brightness. She sank onto the bed and got a surprise when she checked the time. It was after ten. She'd slept four hours and was now wide awake.

Aubrey's stomach rumbled, so she decided to search out the kitchen for some food. When she opened her door, she saw she could navigate by the hall light, so she closed her door behind her. After finding the bathroom across the hall, and with no idea what other bedrooms were on this floor, she tiptoed downstairs and through the quiet house.

Proud of herself for finding the kitchen without taking a wrong turn, she scanned around for some food and was surprised to find a folded piece of paper, with *Aubrey Gannet* written in bold strokes on the front, lying on the counter.

Ms. Gannet,

There are leftovers in the fridge and a microwave beside it. Help yourself. And stay away from that horse.

Beck

Nothing else. Aubrey turned the page over. Blank. No apology. No, "Welcome to the ranch." Just a missive to eat.

Ire rose up within her all over again, at Mara for sending her there, and Beck for, well, for being Beck. The man was more arrogant than anyone Aubrey had ever met. Apparently, it was his way or the highway. First thing tomorrow, she'd take that highway right back home. This had been a colossal mistake.

She found the plate and stuck it in the microwave, watching it circle and imagining her hands rotating around his neck. Except her hands had a mind of their own and instead, they traveled over straight shoulders to a sculpted chest, then around to his back, making his muscles bunch and relax as she moved.

Ding! Aubrey shook herself, grabbed her food and a glass of water and sat at the rectangular table in the center of the large kitchen. She shoved a forkful of casserole in her mouth, drawing circles on the retro-green Formica with her other hand. No way was she attracted to Beck. Who cared that his rugged features fit this life so well. That a small scar on his chin made her want to ask how he got it.

Slowly, the bite she chewed got her attention. This was good. Some sort of chicken, broccoli, and noodle thing, but with complex flavors she couldn't begin to sort out. She liked to cook and considered herself somewhat of a connoisseur, but this was leaps beyond her abilities. After another bite she still had no idea of the spices, so she gave up wondering what they were and enjoyed the rest of her meal. Between this food and meeting Cassidy, Aubrey had finally found something about this ranch that made her smile.

She took her time eating, relishing each bite, wishing she had a nice Sauvignon Blanc to pair with it. Water would have to do for now. When she finished, she rinsed her plate. The dishes in the dishwasher looked clean, so she left hers in the sink, crumpled the note, and threw it in the garbage.

Maybe she could find a book to read. She wandered around but saw nothing that looked like a library. She chose not to open the two closed doors she'd come across. Instead, she stepped outside. Leaning on the porch railing, she drew in a deep breath. Somehow, the whole horse and hay thing didn't seem so strong out here. The lack of car fumes was nice. She missed the noise, though. The absolute quiet unnerved her. A huffing sound caught her attention and she turned to the pasture. Rudy stood at the fence closest to her, watching her.

Even from here, in the dim light, she saw the tortured look in his eyes, and it tore at her. Rudy was a lost soul, just like her. Instinct nudged her heart to help, except that wasn't what she'd come here for. She needed to heal herself before she could help anyone or anything else. Still, the pull was strong. The horse needed her, begged her with his sad eyes.

Aubrey gave in and stepped off the porch. Before she took another step, movement caught her eye. A shadow shifted at the edge of her vision. A small silhouette, heading directly for Rudy. Was it an animal? A coyote or something? Was Rudy in danger?

Her whole body trembling, Aubrey walked with a slow and measured pace toward the horse, probably the most idiotic thing she'd ever done. If he got injured, though, she'd never forgive herself. The shadow disappeared under the fence, but Rudy showed no alarm. He stood there calmly, waiting. When the shadow stopped next to him, the barn light hit it just enough for Aubrey to see what it was. A young child.

Rudy lowered his head toward the child. Beck's stories about bitten men roared up within Aubrey and her heart hit her throat so hard she barely managed to scream.

"No!"

Rudy startled and took off running across the pasture, giving Aubrey time to climb the fence and grab the child. "Oh, my God. Are you all right?" She held the struggling child tight to her chest and climbed the fence, or tried to. Her burden was too ungainly, and she didn't have the strength to boost herself up.

Lights flooded the area and the front door slammed open. Beck, gloriously shirtless, ran out, rifle in hand. He scanned the area.

"Help!"

His gaze whipped her way. Setting the rifle down, he strode toward her, a bundle of angry muscles bunching with each step. "Didn't I tell you to stay away from that damn horse?"

"I didn't plan this," she spat back. "How can you let a

child walk around unattended in the dark of night?"

Beck froze a step from the fence. "A child?"

"Yes, and I can't get over this fence holding this bundle."

Beck's eyes widened when he saw the bundle she held. "Follow me to the gate."

Gate? Aubrey hadn't even thought of that. Quickly through, she hugged the child tight.

"Hand her to me," Beck said.

"Her?"

"Just hand her over."

Aubrey held the child until Beck had her solidly in his arms.

Without a word, Beck turned and walked toward the house, the child cocooned in his arms. Aubrey brushed herself off and followed at a slower pace, wondering who the child belonged to. Beck? That made no sense. Nothing she'd seen so far in his demeanor qualified him as father material.

Inside, Beck was already on the couch with the girl in his lap. From the size of her, she looked to be about six.

"What were you doing? I told you," Beck said. "Never go out at night, and absolutely never get near that horse." He gripped the girl's arm. Aubrey hoped not as hard as he'd gripped hers scant hours earlier.

The girl sniffled. Aubrey saw her lower lip wobbling from across the room, but not much more. The girl's hair obscured most of her face.

Something in that whimper gave Aubrey pause. She'd heard it before. Seen that blond hair before. Had even combed— "Dani?"

Girl and man turned in unison to stare at Aubrey.

"Dani!" she said again, rushing toward her.

Dani screamed and buried her head in Beck's neck, her

hands going white, she clung so tight. Her sniffles became full-on wails.

"Dani, it's me, Aubrey. It's all right, sweetie."

But as Aubrey got closer, Dani's cries increased.

"Back up," Beck said.

Aubrey froze. How could a man speak so quietly and with such force at the same time? He was right, though. As distraught as she herself was, Dani, for reasons she couldn't fathom, was worse. Aubrey moved back to the door.

"It's all right, Dani," Beck soothed, his voice transformed from authority figure to gentle giant. "I've got you. I won't let anything, or anyone,"—he glanced up at Aubrey—"hurt you." He combed her hair with his hands and kept the words up, soft and slow, anything to soothe her.

"Would you mind waiting in the kitchen while I get my niece back to bed?"

At first, his words didn't register. Aubrey thought he still spoke to Dani. When they did, she said, "Oh, yes. Sure, I can do that."

She was halfway to the kitchen when it hit her. He'd called Dani his niece. That meant he was Hope's never-there brother.

CHAPTER THREE

Beck carried the trembling Dani upstairs, hugging her tight. It about tore his heart out to see her so upset. Cassidy stood at the top, worry evident in her clear brown eyes.

"Everything's all right," Beck told her. "Dani went into Rudy's corral."

"Oh, my Lord."

"Go back to sleep. I'll get Dani to bed."

"You want me to do that?"

"No. I need to make sure she's calm, and asleep, before I'll be able to relax."

"Okay, boss. Call me if you need me."

Cassidy disappeared back into her bedroom across the hall from Dani, having chosen to stay in the ranch house instead of at her father's because of the child. Beck was grateful for her help. Beck shouldered Dani's door open and laid his niece on the four-poster, princess-pink, canopied bed he'd bought for her shortly after they'd moved there. The bed he couldn't seem to get her to stay in.

Her crying subsided to sniffles, thank goodness. He settled her under the covers and tucked her in twice, just like his mother had done to him. She seemed to like it.

"Honey, what got you so upset when you saw the lady?" he asked, keeping his voice calm.

Big tears filled the girl's eyes. She crawled out from under the covers and into his arms, clinging to him like it was the last time she'd ever see him.

Beck held her tight, soothing her with the words she wouldn't use, rubbing her back like a soft brush against a horse's skin. Slow strokes, gentle, relaxing. It was all he knew to do.

It took a while, along with a lot more assurances, before he settled Dani back in bed and she dropped off to sleep. Beck closed her door quietly behind him and leaned against the wall. He raked his hair with both hands, at a loss about what had upset his niece. Maybe Aubrey understood? She clearly knew Dani, which meant they needed to talk, and now. This had been one of the most confusing nights he could remember. Almost as bad as the day he'd gotten that phone call.

Dani had been frightened tonight. Scared to death. Why?

Beck had immediately recognized the scream from outside as Aubrey's and his blood had flash-frozen and boiled over at the same time. If she'd gone to that horse ...

He pushed off the wall and headed for the kitchen, then detoured to the office and poured a shot of whiskey, needing the fortification. The woman infuriated him, yet there was something about her that drew him in. A demeanor, a look. And that body of hers sang to his like some goddamned siren song.

One shot of alcohol wasn't enough, but it would have to do. He needed some wits about him to get the answers he needed. Somehow, he didn't think Aubrey Gannet would be in a cooperative mood.

~~~

Aubrey hugged the hot cup of tea. Even with the warm night, cold had seeped into her bones. Only the stove light illuminated the kitchen. Aubrey didn't care, staring into her cup as she reviewed what had happened. The little girl she'd wanted to take in as her own, whom she'd searched for everywhere, was right here. Dani was here. How? And when she'd seen her with Rudy she panicked. But Dani was safe in her bedroom now. Relief replaced the rush of fear that churned in Aubrey's gut. She'd found Dani.

With Beck. Granted, Hope had mentioned him before, but only once. She'd never said anything about Dani being raised by the brother, and Aubrey had a hard time believing she'd have done that. Somehow, the courts must have made that choice.

Aubrey gripped her cup, but no amount of heat cut the chill that snaked through her. Dani, being raised by the brother who hadn't cared enough about Hope to come visit her, even during her final days. The brother who'd made Aubrey so angry, an anger she'd been forced to swallow to help Hope through those terrible hours.

And if he was Hope's brother, that meant—

All the blood in Aubrey's face drained as the cold, hard truth set in. Beck was Mara's cousin. Her friend had sent her here, to the home of a man she could never respect, on purpose. She had to get Dani away from here.

What had she been thinking?

Aubrey would have to deal with Mara later. Right now, she needed out of there. She refused to sleep under the
~~~

same roof as Beck Hawthorne. She didn't give a crap that it was the middle of the night. It was time to get off this ranch. She'd fight to get Dani away from here once she could talk to the girl's social worker. No way would she leave that darling child in the hands of the cold, unfeeling Beck Hawthorne.

Aubrey took her cup to the sink and dumped the tea down the drain, plotting her escape. There wasn't any packing to do. She'd grab her suitcase and purse and leave. Before she reached the kitchen doorway, she froze as the swinging door moved inward. With no other exit that she could see except the window, she gripped the table, white-knuckled with panic. She had to get out of there. She couldn't be there, with him. Not after what he'd done.

Any chance was lost as the door swung wide and Beck strode in, finding her easily in the dim light.

Always insightful about others' emotions, Aubrey saw the raw pain in Beck, a mixture of fear and some of that anger of his adding to his confusion. Aubrey didn't care. This wasn't about him. This was about the pain he'd caused Hope, and about Dani.

"How could you?" She advanced on him, her hands fisted.

Beck took a step back.

Aubrey didn't give him a chance. She swung for the chin again. This time, he deflected it, capturing her fist in his much bigger one.

"Not catching me off guard again, sweetheart."

Having excelled in her self-defense classes, Aubrey didn't hesitate, her other fist connecting with a stomach covered in rock-solid muscle. Beck barely flinched, but the whoosh of air from his lungs meant she'd gotten his attention.

He loosened his grip.

She put everything she had behind her next uppercut. Before she connected again, Beck's arm came up, deflecting her momentum, nudging her back until the wall stopped her. He covered her body with his, making it impossible for her to hit him, or to escape.

They stood there, both breathing hard, for way too long. Aubrey had to look up a ways to glare at him, surprised to see his eyes not connecting with hers. Instead, his gaze lingered on her lips. She licked them, breaking the spell.

"You need to stop hitting me." He whispered the words. His breath, warm and whiskey-flavored, taunted her. Everything pressed against her was hard. Everything.

"Let me go."

"Not until you promise you won't swing for me again. Unless, of course, you want to tussle another way?"

Her body reacted in ways she didn't want it to. No. She was angry with him. Aubrey pushed against his immovable chest, recognizing defeat. "I won't hit you."

With a reluctance Aubrey didn't quite fathom, he backed up. Even more confusing was her reaction to the loss of his heat.

With a thunk, Beck sank to a chair. Elbows on the table, he raked his hands through his hair, grabbing his head like it hurt.

Good.

Aubrey moved slowly around to the far side of the table, leaning against the counter, creating some distance. Beck's shoulders bowed as if he carried a great weight. Guilt, most likely.

When he raised his head, the bleakness in his eyes tugged at her empathy.

You can ease his pain.

Steeling herself against those emotions, Aubrey hugged

herself, trying to keep her sensitive nature at bay.

"Who are you?" he asked. "And, more important, why is my niece so afraid of you?"

Dani's fear toward her lanced Aubrey's heart with pain and her anger disappeared. She'd been wondering about that, too. They'd been good together for those months during her mother's illness. Aubrey used to bring coloring books on her visits and always took time to color a page or two with Dani. The little girl had been so strong through Hope's ordeal. She'd been amazing.

"I don't know."

Beck cocked his head.

"Seriously. We were friends when I last saw her. At least, I thought we were."

"Who are you?" Beck asked again.

Aubrey took a deep breath. "I'm a home-health oncology social worker."

Only the occasional drip from the kitchen faucet broke the silence.

"You were Hope's social worker?"

"I was Hope's friend. And I can't stay here any longer. I refuse to be anywhere near the person who deserted her when she needed him the most."

Beck's face crumpled in on itself, as if the statement alone had slapped him, leaving an imprint of pain behind. Aubrey closed her heart, buried it deep. He needed to hurt. Needed to feel the pain he'd caused Hope.

He covered it quickly. "You know nothing about me."

"You're right. I don't. And, to be honest, I don't want to know anything. I don't want to understand. I just want to be gone."

She marched around the table, intent on getting as far away from him as possible, her anger front and center again.

Beck stood, barring her access to the door. "You can't leave tonight."

Aubrey huffed, straightening to make her not-so-tall stature seem more formidable. "I will leave if I want to."

Beck took a step toward her. He stopped when Aubrey raised her fists and held up his hands, palms out. "It's dangerous, driving around here after dark. If you want to leave, fine. But not until morning."

He stepped back beyond the door. Aubrey glared at him for a moment, then rushed past him and straight for her room. In the time it took her to race up the stairs, reason got through. His was the second caution she'd gotten today about driving at night. Damn it.

Inside her bedroom, she leaned against the closed door and sank to the floor. She couldn't stay there, not knowing what she knew. She'd never sleep a wink. A war raged inside. Physical safety or mental sanity, those were her choices.

Finally, she rose and reached for her suitcase.

Sanity had won the battle. Aubrey was leaving.

CHAPTER FOUR

Beck made his decision in about thirty seconds. Aubrey Gannet was a stubborn woman with a mind of her own, and she'd ignore his warning. She would leave. He headed out the door. In front of the porch, he picked up a couple of wood slivers.

"Not until morning, when it's safe."

Crouching beside her car, he unscrewed the air cap on the tire valve and pushed in the twig. A satisfying hiss answered him. He did a second tire, then strode around the house and in through the side door before she could see him. She'd figure it out. She was smart like that. But it still meant she'd be here in the morning. Safe.

Once inside his office, Beck sank into his chair, leaving the light off. He could see well enough with the drapes open.

She'd been there for Hope when he should have been. Remorse, never far from his heart, gutted him like physical pain. He leaned his forearms on his knees, letting the pain wash over him, his penance for being so self-centered. To feel the pain of his rejection of Hope every hour of every day, though Hope had never told her why. To know how badly he'd hurt his flesh and blood, his only sibling. The only family he had left except for Mara. And Dani.

Hope's note, attached to her will, had been short and to the point.

I think Dani will be as good for you as you will be for her. Don't let her forget me.

That's why he'd named the ranch after Hope. For Dani, and to make sure he always remembered what he'd done. To make sure he paid for his mistakes. A lifetime would not assuage his shame.

"I'm so sorry, Hope."

Reaching for the whiskey, Beck caught his reflection in a mirror lit by refracted moonlight. He saw eyes reddened by his stoic attempt to keep the tears at bay. Skin deeply lined by guilt. He scrubbed at the scruff he usually shaved off, the tactile roughness somehow soothing him. Maybe he'd keep the beard.

Downing the shot he'd poured, Beck stared out the window at the car that stood silent, two tires flattened. What was he going to do about Aubrey Gannet?

Speaking of which, he'd been right.

She stepped off the porch, glanced back at the house, then walked to her car. She raised the trunk lid, then stepped around to open the driver's door, plunking herself into the seat. She started the engine, drove about twenty feet, then got back out of the car, staring at the two tires he'd deflated.

"Arrgggghhhhh!" she screamed. She turned to the house and glared directly at his office window.

Uncharacteristically, Beck sank back into his chair.

This argument was best left for daylight. At least, that's what he told himself as Aubrey yanked her suitcase back out and pounded her way into the house.

It was a long time before Beck found the courage to head to his own room.

~~~

Aubrey spent very little of the night asleep. A good part had been filled with silent ranting at the authoritarian attitude of one Beck Hawthorne. At some point, while she tossed and turned, she'd entertained the fear she should have felt long before. The man had anger issues and had flattened her tires. What else would he do? Except Mara wouldn't put her in harm's way. Ever. She trusted that instinct. Eventually, the real reason for her emotional upheaval sank in. Dani.

Finding Dani seemed like a God-sent gift. Aubrey still couldn't believe the child was there, of all places. If Mara had known where Dani had disappeared to, why hadn't she told Aubrey? Mara should have known anything to do with Hope was important to Aubrey. She'd be having a long talk with her friend when she had cell service again.

A solution to the mess still eluded Aubrey, even after hours of thought and zero sleep. She couldn't leave Dani there with Beck. He'd been so careful with the child last night that Aubrey knew, instinctively, he wouldn't hurt Dani. But the man was cold and unfeeling, so different from the vibrancy of his sister. Dani deserved more than Beck's austere view of life. Yet, with the girl fearful of her, what could she do? What had changed to make the child terrified of her?

Aubrey had never been so unsure of her course of action. Beck had custody of Dani, so child services must be involved. If she found out who the caseworker was, she might be able to plead her case. At least the caseworker
~~~

would be aware Dani had options.

How could she continue to be part of the child's life, to help her through the grief of losing her mother? Staying on the ranch wasn't an option since Beck came along with that prospect. He'd deserted her friend and no reason could justify it. Yet, she'd glimpsed something last night. A hint that he had demons of his own. There were stories there, and bringing those stories out, starting the healing process, that was Aubrey's specialty.

She also had to acknowledge the reason she'd come to the ranch. She'd depleted herself. She didn't have the strength to help anyone except Dani. Why had Mara sent her to this place? She must have thought being here would be good for her, maybe even for Dani and Beck. But Aubrey couldn't do it. She'd destroy what little of herself was left if she stayed.

She had to leave. Today. Once back in Butte, she'd check with local agencies, try to find Dani's caseworker and let her know she'd raise the girl in a heartbeat.

Sunlight streamed through the window. Aubrey walked over and pulled the curtain back, surprised to see Beck airing up her tires with a portable generator. Seemed he had meant it about keeping her safe. She watched him, his muscles flexing through his gray t-shirt, and an unfamiliar warmth filled her. This kindness hit right where she didn't need it. Her heart softened against her will. She yanked the curtains closed and turned away. She didn't want to like Beck Hawthorne. The man was gruff and overpowering.

Though she hadn't made the best first impression herself, had she? Maybe she should make more of an effort to be civil. For Dani's sake.

In the bathroom, she ran water in the basin, splashing it over her face, trying to ease the weariness she felt. Her reflection in the mirror didn't even look like her. Deep shadows beneath her eyes told of sleepless nights, and her cheekbones were more prominent than ever. Her skin, something she'd always been so careful to preserve, looked sallow and sickly. Aubrey ran a hand through limp, brown hair in dire need of new color. A full inch showed her need for updated highlights.

How had she let herself get this bad? Aubrey shook her head. She'd take better care of herself once she settled this thing with Dani.

Back in her room, she picked up her belongings and went downstairs. The smell of food, yummy food, waited for her at the bottom. Maybe breakfast wasn't a bad idea. Fortification before she spoke with Beck and got on the road. Because somewhere between her room and the bottom of the steps, she'd decided that it was only fair to tell Beck that she intended to fight for custody of Dani.

Nodding, resolved, Aubrey set her suitcase near the door and walked down the hall to the kitchen. The smells got stronger and now she heard voices. Aubrey turned at a doorway to find the dining room.

"Ah, there you are," Cassidy said, coming in from another door. "Breakfast is about over. I was just coming to wake you."

Aubrey returned the young woman's welcoming smile. "Hi, Cassidy."

"Call me Cassie. Everyone does. Well, everyone except Beck. Who knows why?" She shook her head as she grabbed Aubrey's arm, pulling her to the table. "Coffee?"

"I'd love some, but I can get it myself."

Cassie waved her hand. "Nah, I'll get it. And I'll tell the cook to get you a plate of food. Do you take anything in your coffee?"

Aubrey shook her head. "Black and leaded."

"Coffee's strong here. You sure? I put white chocolate

peppermint creamer in mine to make it palatable." She leaned in conspiratorially. "Don't tell the cook that, though. He doesn't take kindly to constructive criticism."

Aubrey laughed. "I'll still take it black, and thanks for the tip."

Cassidy slid back through the door, leaving Aubrey alone in the dining room. She sat in one of the straight-backed chairs and looked around. The entire ranch must breakfast here, if the stacks of dishes showing a well-eaten meal were any indication. A long slab of wood with a live edge on both sides made for a beautiful table. She ran her hands over the wood. There was a buffet against one wall, its wood similar in color to the table but with a more formal design to it. A few paintings hung on the walls, different aspects of ranch life, all very well done. A local artist? An elaborate "C" in the lower right corner gave the only clue to the artist. Aubrey turned to look at the picture behind her and caught her breath. Hope!

She stood and moved closer to the painting. The artist had captured her smiling, though Aubrey guessed Hope was a few years younger in this picture than when they knew each other. She touched the frame as a few tears slid over her cheeks. God, but she missed her friend. The first time she'd met her, Hope had told her in no uncertain terms that if she planned to feel sorry or sad for her, she should just leave and send someone else. "Only happiness resides in my house," she'd said.

The smallest noise turned Aubrey's head. She wasn't even sure she'd heard anything, but there, at the edge of the room, something moved. No. Someone. A small someone. Dani?

Aubrey moved slowly to the table and sat down. "I won't hurt you, Dani," she said. "I'd love to talk to you, but only if you want to." She kept her voice quiet and low, not wanting to spook the girl. For the life of her, she didn't understand why Dani was afraid. She'd done nothing but try to help her, and it broke Aubrey's heart that Dani now feared her.

CHAPTER FIVE

Saying that he'd take the coffee to Aubrey, Beck sent Cassidy out with a thermos to the workers who'd been busy since shortly after sun up. He froze in the doorway when he saw Dani in the corner of the dining room.

And Aubrey at the table.

Dani's eyes, big and round, were worried. But she didn't bolt, brave girl.

Aubrey spoke to her in soothing tones, not trying to get closer, giving her time to get used to Aubrey being there. Smart. He admired those instincts.

Dani looked so vulnerable, so sad and afraid. Beck had tried to get through to the girl, but to date, he'd never once heard her speak. It surprised him how much he wanted Dani's voice to fill the house. More than anything, he wanted her to be happy. That fierce need caught him off guard, because Beck had never considered himself father material. Hell, he'd screwed up being a brother. How would he ever be a dad?

"I remember how much you loved to color," Aubrey said.

Beck nodded. That remained her favorite pastime. Well, when she wasn't out ranging the ranch with him, or trying to get to that damn horse.

"Do you still color?"

No answer.

"Animals. That's what you colored the most," Aubrey continued. "And you were good at it. Always tried to stay within the lines unless you didn't like something. Then you'd draw your own line."

Beck smiled. He'd seen Dani do that, and it had taken a while to understand why.

"Now that I know you're here, I'll get you some of those special books I used to bring you. Do you remember those?"

Dani watched Aubrey closely. That she hadn't taken off was a pretty big deal. She didn't stick around strangers at all, but she had a history with Aubrey. From what Aubrey indicated, they'd shared a good relationship. Beck didn't understand why fear had muddled that, but maybe everything was tied together. Hope, Aubrey, Dani. Even himself.

Once Beck had been informed that Hope selected him to be Dani's guardian, he'd bought the ranch and moved them there. Mara had come to stay until they'd found a routine. Now, Mara had sent him Aubrey, another person in pain. To help? Was it that simple? There would be no healing for Beck's kind of pain, but maybe, just maybe, Aubrey might flush out the grief whirling around inside Dani's head and heart.

He'd do whatever was necessary to return Dani to happiness. She'd been happy before. Mara had told him that. In the five months Dani had been under his care, he'd failed miserably. Sure, she ate. She went through the machinations of the day, coloring, following him around the ranch. But there was no reason for her to remain silent. That had to be emotional.

He didn't like Aubrey being here or that Mara had sent her. His cousin had manipulated him. Beck had never tolerated manipulation well. For Dani, though …

Decision made, Beck stepped into the room. Dani, so focused on Aubrey, spooked and took off. He'd find her in his office, at her little table, coloring. Her safe place.

Aubrey turned to him, eyes full of accusation. Flecks of white ice lightened the blue when anger filled them. It entranced him.

Mentally shaking himself, he set the cup he held down on the table in front of her. "Coffee. Cream and sugar are there." He pointed down the table. "Breakfast will be ready in a couple minutes."

Those delicious eyes widened. "You're the cook?"

"Yep." He nodded. "Cook, horse-herder, stall-mucker, though I do wash my hands after that chore."

Her glimmer of a smile got his attention. The corners of her lips lifted the tiniest bit, the hint of a dimple making him want to see more. He cleared his throat. "Anyhow, be right back."

He hurried back to the kitchen to get her eggs going before his heart scrambled his brain. He did not have time for this. For her.

Returning shortly, he set a plate full of eggs, bacon, and toast in front of her, then sat across the table with his own cup of coffee.

"It's, ummm, rather a lot of food," Aubrey said.

Beck shrugged. "We eat light lunches here, so I'm used to loading the morning plates. Eat what you want. The rest will go into scrap buckets for the pigs."

"You have pigs?"

"Pigs, chickens, horses, a stray dog or two, and lots of cats. One of Dani's jobs is to gather eggs each morning."

"Isn't she too young?"

"Not at all. I collected eggs daily from the time I was four. Would have done it earlier, but apparently, I thought it was funny to throw the eggs to the ground and watch them go splat."

There it was again, the hint of a dimple, quashed when she sucked in her lower lip. Beck couldn't tell if it was continued ire or to keep her from laughing, but chose to believe the latter.

"I can imagine that's not conducive to a breakfast plate like this."

"Eat while it's warm."

Aubrey picked up a piece of bacon and bit into it, closing her eyes as her lips closed around it. "Mmm."

Beck raised an eyebrow.

"Good," she said, chewing. "Really good."

"Then eat."

Aubrey dug in with a gusto unexpected for someone so thin. Beck watched her enjoy the food, wondering what else she liked. And suddenly, he wanted answers to that question.

"I'm still mad at you," Aubrey said.

He held his arms wide. "I aired up your tires first thing."

"Kind of makes it hard to stay mad, but I'm trying."

"I won't apologize. I know the dangers on these roads. You don't."

"You didn't even give me the chance to make my own choice."

"Ah, but you did. You chose to scream."

Her flush of red was absolutely adorable. There was no stoic restraint to this girl who wore her emotions on her face. He liked that about her. She might not like him much, but at least he knew where he stood.

"All right," she said, after glaring at him. "I concede. I did try to leave last night."

"And I made it possible for you to leave first thing this morning if you wanted, once daylight came."

Aubrey nodded, taking a bite of toast slathered in peach jam.

"But I hope you'll stay."

Aubrey choked on the bread, coughing so much Beck almost came around the table to pound her on the back. He poured a glass of water and pushed it toward her. Once she calmed enough to take a drink, Aubrey wiped her mouth with her napkin and stared at Beck. For the first time, her face was a mask devoid of emotion.

"Why?" she finally asked. "You didn't exactly welcome me with open arms yesterday."

Should he tell her this was all about Dani? In the end, letting that happen organically might be better. "You seem to have a way with Rudy."

"The horse?"

"Yes."

"I don't think— "

"Hear me out."

She pursed those sweet lips of hers, nodding.

"I'm not used to asking for help, but no one's been able to get near him. He's a filthy mess. Thank God he eats, or we'd have had to put him down. But I can't reach him. No one can. If you and I worked together, maybe you'll be able to convince him I'm a nice guy."

Aubrey huffed. "I'm not so sure myself, yet."

"Hey. I made you breakfast."

"And it is very good. But breakfast alone does not make for a nice guy." She rubbed her arm.

"Did I hurt you yesterday?" Beck reached over to lift her sleeve and look at her arm, realized he was being too familiar, and pulled his hand back.

"No bruises, thank you. You do have a strong grip, though."

Damn. Hurting women was not his thing and never would be. He leaned closer, made sure he had eye contact with her. "I'm sorry. That was not my intention."

"I get that." Aubrey sucked in a breath. "And thank you. I accept your apology."

"Then you'll help with Rudy?"

"I'm not sure my being here is a good idea, Beck." She glanced behind her at the empty doorway. The doorway Dani had dashed through moments earlier.

He saw the pain in her drawn face and knew that was a tough admission for her. He could appreciate that.

"You have an attachment to my niece. It would give you more time with her." Beck had shot the last ammo he had. He mentally crossed his fingers that it would help Aubrey decide.

"I don't know," she said, watching him with those wounded eyes of hers, making him want to wipe away her concerns.

He tried. "Can you see that everything I've done has been to protect Dani, and that I was only trying to keep you safe last night, and with the horse?"

She nodded.

"Then why not give it a try." Beck spread his arms. "I'm harmless. Really."

That hint of dimple returned, maybe even a touch deeper, and settled in him like a sip of warmed whiskey, going down smooth with a lot of feel-good pulled behind.

"Can I take some time to think about it?"

"Definitely." Time to think meant more time spent here on the ranch. "Eat your breakfast. I'm heading out to the barn. Dani will be with me, so take all the time you need." He placed his hand over hers, hoping it wasn't too much. "Please don't leave without telling me. I promise to be back here by noon, so if you've decided to leave, you'll have plenty of time to get back to Butte before dark."

Aubrey stared at their hands, sucking in that lower lip of hers. Beck reacted in a way he should not be reacting, so he pulled his hand back.

When she nodded, he let out the breath he'd been holding and stood. He needed to get out of there before she saw how she affected him. "Thank you," he said. "Just put the dishes in the sink when you're done. I can meet you in my office at noon. First door to the left at the front of the house."

He walked out, trying very hard not to let this momentary truce between them give him hope. At least, not yet.

~~~

After Beck left, Aubrey sipped her coffee, holding the cup in both hands to let the remaining warmth seep into her. Beck Hawthorne didn't like the word no. With those piercing eyes and a body honed by ranch chores, she'd found it difficult to flat-out refuse, though she should have. Staring at him seemed much more enjoyable, and that needed to stop now. Dani's future was at stake, and an attraction to the man she considered unsuitable to raise the child only complicated matters. Aubrey's plan to leave remained the best option.

She finished her breakfast, rinsed her dishes, and put them in the dishwasher. With nothing to do except think, Aubrey headed outside and sat on the top step, still unsure.
~~~

If she stayed, she would be close to Dani. She could get to know her again and try to figure out why the child reacted to her the way she did. If she left, she had a better chance of finding Dani's caseworker to let him or her know other options were available for Dani's care. She'd be more comfortable with her surroundings and have more control over, well, everything.

Rudy watched her from the edge of his corral. Aubrey looked around to make certain no one would bushwhack her this time before walking over. Beck couldn't be annoyed since he'd asked her to work with Rudy, right? She reached for his nose. The horse showed little hesitation. He didn't back up, didn't shiver, nothing. In fact, he reached toward her hand, nudging her as they touched. His hair was coarse and dirty, but Aubrey didn't care. As soon as she touched him, everything else fell away except the two of them, bonding through shared pain. The emotional scars inside Rudy hit Aubrey like a physical manifestation. Her empathy swelled, and she hurt for him. Someone had done him harm, and pain was pain. There was a kindred soul inside this horse, an injured spirit that spoke to her.

She reached up to run her hand along his neck. Rudy leaned into her touch. They stood there together, locked in shared pain. Aubrey's tears wet Rudy's hair, and he huffed softly in response.

When she pulled back to wipe her cheeks, she took a good long look at him. He didn't seem tense, though Aubrey's horse knowledge was minimal at best. His ears were forward, focused on her, his nostrils weren't flared, and his jaw looked slack, not tight. So it seemed he could relax, but not around Beck or his men. Which meant, if he'd been abused, it must have been by a man.

"We're two peas in a pod, aren't we, Rudy? Unable to find a way back from the edge."

He nickered, nodding his head a couple times. Aubrey smiled, rubbing his nose, knowing that her fate had been decided. Rudy needed her. Dani needed her. She wouldn't leave them. And that was okay, because somewhere, deep down inside, she knew that in helping them, she might find her own way out of the darkness.

So be it.

"I'm staying, boy. We'll have time together, you and I."

Rudy's tail lifted and he tossed his head with a soft neigh.

Aubrey headed back to the house in a lighter mood, intent on grabbing another cup of that great coffee and going up to her room to settle in.

CHAPTER SIX

Beck waited until Aubrey went inside before he stepped out from the side of the house. It had taken every ounce of willpower to not rush over and keep her away from that horse. When she'd reached out, Beck was convinced Rudy would bite her. Instead, the damn horse had welcomed her touch. Welcomed it. It didn't seem to matter who fed him, who made sure he had shelter from weather and sunshine, who'd brought him there to rescue him from a tough situation. No. The horse had chosen Aubrey. Thank goodness he'd left Dani with Cassidy. If she'd seen Aubrey with Rudy, there'd be no controlling her desire to be near that horse.

Though Beck had always been good with horses, Rudy tried every bit of his patience. If Aubrey stayed, maybe she could help Rudy and him find a working relationship. He'd sure like to help the horse.

Damaged souls. That's what filled this ranch. And

Beck had no idea how to help any of them, let alone himself. Here less than a day, Aubrey had already become pivotal to solving at least two of Beck's problems. He didn't understand it, and he sure as hell didn't know how to interpret it. When he spent time with her, he wanted to smile. Wanted to reach for some of that happiness he didn't deserve.

He walked to the opposite side of the corral and watched the horse. Rudy stared back with wary eyes. As soon as Beck put a hand on the top rail, the horse pulled his head back and followed the opposite side of the corral to the furthest point from Beck.

It was the damnedest thing Beck had ever seen. A brown-and-white horse with a black-and-white attitude. And he'd made his choice.

So be it. Now all he had to do was convince Aubrey to stay and help. He hoped he'd already done that. In fact, he figured that, with that good heart of hers, she'd be unable to resist helping Rudy and Dani. Beck would bet his ranch she'd decide to stay and that lightened his heart. For some reason, he no longer felt alone. This was a foreign emotion for him. He'd need some time to decide if he liked it or not.

Beck turned back toward the barn to finish the last stall he needed to update before he brought in more horses to kick-start the breeding program. He'd been looking at mares for weeks and had a couple in mind, as well as a stallion or two. Once everything was in place, they'd move to stage two of making Hope Ranch a viable business and a permanent home where he could raise Dani.

In the end, that was all that mattered.

~~~

Settling in didn't take Aubrey long and left her with an hour to fill until she met with Beck. She wondered about the wifi situation. If she could tap that, she could use her
~~~

laptop to reach Mara and do some research. Better yet, maybe she'd ask to use the house phone. She expected her conversation with Mara to be a long one, and she wanted to hear her friend's remorse instead of trying to squeeze it out of some emotionless email response. Of course, this assumed Mara would be remorseful.

Back downstairs, Aubrey wandered around the house, familiarizing herself. She knew the kitchen, and the cook, for that matter. The dining room led to the front room and the main door. The door opposite was closed. Aubrey opened it and peeked inside.

Reclaimed wood paneling covered the wall behind a massive dark desk. She smiled at the toddler-size desk dwarfed by the bigger one and covered in crayons and coloring books.

Two other walls were light-colored, textured sheetrock, and the fourth held floor to ceiling bookshelves. She perused the section on ranch law, breeding, and financial bookkeeping and stopped in front of several trophies. Rodeo trophies. Aubrey picked one up. They weren't for bronc or bull-riding. They were for being a rodeo clown. They gave trophies for that? She tried to picture the formidable Beck staring down a Brahma bull in clown makeup and red clothes.

No matter how much she tried, she couldn't stop giggling at the image.

When the doorbell rang, Aubrey bobbled the trophy and almost dropped it. Setting it back on the shelf with her heart pounding, she exited the office, closed the door, and, since no one else had shown up, opened the front door.

A petite older woman stood there in jeans, cowboy boots, and a white t-shirt covered by a southwestern motif long-sleeved shirt. Her silver hair gleamed, matching her smile.

"May I help you?" Aubrey asked.

"I'm here to see Beckett Hawthorne?"

Aubrey looked around, aware that Beck was not in the house. "He's, umm, probably out on the ranch somewhere."

The woman laughed. "I get that a lot. It comes with this territory." She held out her hand. "I'm Laura Castillo, social services."

"Oh," Aubrey said, thrilled to have this gift drop into her lap. "You must be Dani's caseworker. Come in, come in."

She shut the door behind Laura and gestured to the front room.

"I am," Laura said. "I'm Dani's court-appointed guardian ad litem. And you are?"

"I'm sorry. My name is Aubrey Gannet. I spent time with Dani before her mother passed away."

"Then you're from the Seattle area?"

"Yes. Umm, can I offer you a beverage or something?"

"I'm fine, thank you."

Laura sat down on the couch and Aubrey took the chair opposite her, her hands tucked beneath her legs.

"How did you know Hope?" Laura asked.

"Through the hospice program. I'm a social worker as well. Hope and I became friends." She drew a deep breath.

Laura cocked her head. "Not the smartest thing to do, becoming attached to a patient."

No argument came to Aubrey's mind. "You're right. It wasn't smart, but Hope had such a way about her. She pulled people in, made them feel special."

"How so?"

"Like, one day, I arrived to find she and Dani had put streamers up everywhere. They had even baked a birthday cake. For me. I'd never mentioned my birthday, but she somehow got hold of the date. Since I'm an only child, and my parents are divorced and both live on the East Coast, Hope and Dani had planned a celebration."

Aubrey looked out the window, awash in memories. Hope had about exhausted herself that day, but the joy it brought her had been worth it.

"It was impossible not to like her, and Dani by extension."

"I'm very happy to meet someone who knew Dani before her life changed so drastically," Laura said, smiling.

"Yes, and I don't understand the change that's come over her. She was vibrant around her mother. Full of laughter and joy, always smiling."

"Grief does that to people. And to a child ... "

"I can't imagine what she's going through. I—I tried to find her, after ... "

"Really? Why?"

"I didn't do my job very well. I not only got attached to Hope, I fell for Dani. I'd hoped to help her through this process, maybe even become her legal guardian. But she disappeared."

Laura watched Aubrey closely. "If you don't mind me asking, how did you find Dani?"

"Through Mara, Hope and Beck's cousin. I've been friends with Mara for a long time. I didn't meet Hope until Mara asked me to help her."

Aubrey wished she and Hope could have been friends long before Hope got sick. All those potential years of friendship wasted, although gratitude for the time they had together overshadowed her regret. She willed her shoulders to relax and released her tightly clutched hands as she waited for Laura to ask her next question. In this business, answers were evidence. Laura seemed nice, but revealing that she was still lost in grief wouldn't help make her a serious candidate for guardianship.

"Then you've come to see if everything is going well for Dani?"

"I need her to be happy."

"Do you think Beck's doing a good job?"

In a way, Aubrey and Beck had entered into a competition and the prize was Dani, but that didn't mean she would be dishonest. In the clear light of day, her earlier conclusions about Beck seemed harsh. She couldn't bring herself to say she knew whether Beck was doing right by Dani. Not yet. "I've been here less than a day, so I don't have a good feel for that."

Laura nodded. "I appreciate that. Have you seen Dani?"

"Yes, I have. A couple of times."

"So you're aware she isn't speaking."

Aubrey nodded, deciding to hold tight about Dani screaming when she first saw Aubrey.

"What was she like, with her mother?"

"Vibrant, talkative, and everything else a normal six-year-old would be." Aubrey smiled, thinking of Dani back then. "She was curious and everything amazed her."

"It's nice to have that perspective."

"She seems to trust Beck. She runs to him first when she needs help," Aubrey said, though that bit of honesty could well hurt her own desire to raise Dani.

"I noticed that, too. There's a bond growing there that rather surprises me." Laura shook her head. "I've known Beck for a lot of years. I knew his parents."

"They lived around here?"

"Around here? Try here. This was their ranch. Beck and Hope sold it after their parents died. The new owners couldn't manage it well enough and it fell into bankruptcy. Beck bought it from the bank right after he got Dani. It was in pretty poor shape."

"Then he's done a lot of work on the place in a short amount of time."

"He has."

Beck was trying hard to make a decent home for Dani. Aubrey respected that because she'd do the same thing if given the chance.

Was now the time? Should she tell Laura she wanted Dani? Beck seemed so authoritarian and was such a stickler for rules. That wasn't how free-spirited Hope had raised Dani. Aubrey didn't know yet if Beck's ranch was the best place for the child. If it wasn't, Aubrey wanted it on record that she would love to raise Dani if given the opportunity. "If I may speak for a moment about Dani's situation."

"Go ahead."

Aubrey took a deep breath. "I'd become Dani's guardian in a heartbeat. It would be dishonest of me, though, if I didn't admit that Beck is trying hard, and Dani looks at him like her lifeline. But if things ever change, please know that I would love to have Dani come live with me."

"Understood. And appreciated," Laura said. "I can see how much you care for Dani. I think it would be good for her to have a woman as a role model, not to mention someone who was so close to her mother. It would be nice if the two of you could work together to bring Dani back to a full and happy life."

Work with Beck? He'd already asked her to work with Rudy and intimated she'd have time with Dani. This vacation wasn't really a vacation at all.

Somewhere in the back of the house, a door opened.

"That's probably Beck now," Aubrey said.

"Good. I can meet with him, hopefully see Dani, then I'll be out of your hair."

"I enjoyed our talk," Aubrey said. She shook Laura's hand.

"I enjoyed it, too. A very enlightening conversation."

CHAPTER SEVEN

"Enlightening?" Beck said, coming around the corner, stopping short when he saw how chummy Aubrey and Dani's guardian ad litem appeared to be. What the hell was so enlightening?

Aubrey stood too quickly for his peace of mind and looked away before she met his eyes. "Laura's here to see you, Beck."

First names? Beck didn't have anything to hide, but the mere idea that Laura could take Dani away from him, for any reason, put a giant sack of grain on his chest, pressing his heart, making it hard to breathe. He loved Dani. It shocked him how fast that had happened, but it was true. He wanted what was best for her. To formally adopt her, take care of her, and find a way inside that shell she'd built around herself. Helping her become the amazing person she was meant to be consumed his heart, his mind, his every waking moment. He was meant to raise her. No one else.

"Surprise visit?" He arched an eyebrow.

Laura smiled, holding out her hand. "I have to throw one or two in to satisfy the court."

Great. Beck shook her hand, then turned his arched eyebrow to Aubrey.

"Well, I'll leave you two to chat." She sidled out of the room, edging along the outskirts until she'd passed him, another cog in his worry wheel.

Beck frowned even as his pulse kicked up watching her walk away. What kind of hell would she put him through just by being here? She might be way more complication than he needed.

"So," he said, sitting down in the chair Aubrey vacated, liking her lingering warmth a little too much. "Have you been here long?"

Laura laughed. "It's all right, Beck. She didn't tell me anything I didn't already know. Relax. I'm on your side. You and Dani are good for each other. It was valuable, though, to get some insight into how Dani was before your sister passed."

Beck suppressed the cringe those words elicited. Even thinking about Hope—that way—made his chest tight. The guilt consumed him. But knowing what Dani was like before? That was an appealing carrot to dangle, and he'd be interested in that information as well.

"Your niece has a ways to go to climb out of her grief."

Beck frowned. "I'm trying to help. I'm not sure how to reach her."

"Maybe," Laura said with a glance at the door, "your new houseguest can help."

Except Dani had run screaming from Aubrey. Beck opted not to tell Laura he'd allowed his niece to be traumatized.

He nodded instead, though the speculation in Laura's gaze worried him.

"She's pretty," Laura said.

"Dani?"

"No. Dani is cute. Aubrey is pretty."

"I hadn't noticed." Actually, Beck wouldn't call her pretty. He'd say beautiful, wholesome, and soul-wrenchingly sad. To him, pretty meant perfect makeup, clothes designed to show off a faultless body, and an attitude to go with it. He knew pretty. He'd seen it time and again in the city. Instinct told him Aubrey was nothing like those women. She'd never go behind his back to manipulate him or his life. Normally, Beck trusted his instincts. But right now, there was too much at stake to trust anybody. And Laura's intuitive smile overflowed with ideas he needed to shut down.

"So, what's up for today's visit?"

"Mostly, I came to see Dani."

"She's with Cassidy at the moment. They fed the chickens and now they're working on writing their letters out in the barn. School starts in a month."

"Good. With what happened to her mother, Dani is behind and will be almost a year older than most of her classmates."

"Exactly. I want to give her the best start possible."

"Sounds perfect, since I've seen your handwriting."

Beck grinned, the last of his concern fading away. "I write well enough to get the point across, but I cook to hide that small flaw in my character. Dani and I read together. She's on second-grade level stuff. Not reading out loud, but she follows along with her finger. And when I say a random word from the page, she points right to it." Beck stood and straightened like a proud father.

"That's great." Laura stood and placed her hand on his

arm like a gentle grandmother. "Just keep doing what you are and everything will fall into place."

"I wish she'd talk," he admitted. "I can't break through that wall, not even to get a goodnight when I put her to bed."

"Time will help her get past that. I don't think there's cause to worry too much yet. It hasn't been that long."

Time. The salve that heals all wounds? Hardly.

"Let me walk you out to the barn," Beck said.

"Thanks."

Aubrey sat on the porch step and jumped up when they went outside.

"Would you like to walk to the barn with us, Aubrey?" Laura asked.

Her gut reaction, a solid no, showed in Aubrey's expressive face. Probably because of the scowl Beck couldn't quite hide.

"Come if you want," he said.

She chewed her lower lip, then nodded.

~~~

They walked in companionable silence across to the barn. Aubrey, mired in worry over that scowl on Beck's face, at first didn't notice her surroundings. What had Laura told him? She'd been foolish to even mention wanting Dani. She shouldn't have put that out there without knowing more about the girl's situation. It wasn't fair to Dani or Beck.

As they walked, the sheer enormity of Beck's ranch grabbed Aubrey's attention. Everywhere she looked was expansive, flat land, edged by drastic rock monuments and hills. It went on forever, with only a building or fence here and there to break the view. The landscape was vast and beautiful, and so foreign that it overwhelmed her.

Aubrey turned in a complete circle, her mouth wide
~~~

open. *Wow.* Beck and Laura both stopped to watch her, amusement on Laura's face and rightful pride on Beck's.

"This place is huge."

Beck chuckled. "We don't do anything small in Montana."

"I can see that."

"Never been to a ranch?" Laura asked.

Aubrey shook her head.

"Well then, welcome to Montana. I've lived here all my life," Laura said, looking around. "Never gets old."

They started walking and Aubrey followed, albeit more slowly as she tried to take it all in. What a difference from Seattle. Nary a skyscraper in sight. Nothing in sight, really, except land, land, and more land.

Inside the barn, she let her eyes adjust to the dimmer light. Laura and Beck walked through a door to the right and Aubrey followed, surprised to see a full office inside. Cassidy and her charge sat at the desk, hunched over some paper on which Dani wrote with studious care. Aubrey could see crude letters. She smiled, happy Dani's education hadn't been forgotten. Hope had loved working with her daughter on her letters. Okay, Hope had loved everything Dani-related.

Dani lifted her head. When she saw Beck, she smiled. Then, when she caught sight of Aubrey, the smile died, hitting Aubrey straight in the heart. Dani raced around the desk and threw herself at Beck, burying her head in his neck.

Beck soothed her with words Aubrey couldn't hear while Laura looked at them all like they were a mystery she intended to solve. It had been a mistake for Aubrey to come with them. Until she had a chance to unravel why Dani had taken a dislike to her, she'd better keep a low profile around the girl's caseworker.

"I'll, um, go check out that scenery some more, if that's all right?"

Beck nodded and Aubrey backed out of the office, breathing a big sigh as she walked down the wide main aisle of the barn, the strong smell of hay both foreign and comforting. She remembered those Saturdays when her mother had taken her to riding lessons. She'd fallen in love with horses back then, though her parent's divorce had put a financial end to that. The stalls were empty of horses at the moment, though she'd seen a few in the distance while driving in yesterday. She wondered if she'd like riding now as much as she used to.

Had it only been yesterday that she'd arrived? Aubrey's emotions had bounced all over the place in such a short amount of time. Managing them while working with Rudy and getting to know Dani again would be a test to her already overtaxed psyche, yet she couldn't turn her back on either of them.

After she made her way to the front of the barn, she headed back toward the house. Rudy stared at her over the fence. Poor guy didn't speak, didn't beg. He just stared at her with those moon-drop sad eyes of his.

She joined him, reaching up to scratch his forehead, absent-mindedly combing through the snarls in his forelock with her fingers.

"We're a fine pair, aren't we? Both overwhelmed by fear. Me, of losing myself helping others. And you ... " She leaned against his nose. Rudy huffed but didn't move. "What are you afraid of, boy? Who hurt you, and how?"

Rudy shivered. At first, Aubrey thought it a reaction to her question, until it grew worse. It didn't take her long to figure it out. She turned to see Beck and Laura walking her way. At least Rudy didn't bolt.

"I get it, boy. He's a force to be reckoned with. I won't

ask you to deal with him. Not today, anyway." She straightened and gave him a final pat. "Go."

Rudy tossed his head in thanks, at least, that's what Aubrey chose to believe. Then he trotted away to the far side of the fence. Aubrey counted it as a win that he hadn't torn up the ground moving off. Maybe Beck was right. Maybe the horse trusted her. Unlike Beck, who clearly did not, and whose scowl indicated she'd be hearing about this later. Aubrey raised her chin. No one had told her what to do in a very long time and she wasn't about to let Beck Hawthorne start handing her orders now.

"I see you've made friends with the beast," Laura said, looking between the two with a bemused expression on her face. "And you, Beck. You let her near that animal?"

"Not by choice."

Laura laughed. "Well, it appears the horse is the one making the choices at the moment."

Aubrey laughed as Beck's scowl deepened.

Laura held out her hand to Aubrey. "It was nice to meet you. I hope I get to see you again." She turned to Beck. "You're doing everything right. Give Dani time and lots of love. That's really all she needs right now. Stability, and arms that will always hold her."

He nodded without speaking, but Aubrey saw the glint of emotion in his eyes.

They watched as Laura got in her car and pulled away. Then Beck faced Aubrey.

"What were you and Laura talking about before I walked in the room?"

So Laura hadn't told him. Aubrey sent a ray of thanks winging toward the social worker. "Just stuff. She wanted to know what Dani was like. You know, before."

"I would like to know that, too."

A rare cloud dimmed the sun and Aubrey's mood

dimmed with it. "If you'd been there, you'd know."

Beck's jaw worked overtime as he tried to get himself under control. He opened his mouth twice, then shut it again. Finally, he got some words out. "Don't get near that horse without me."

Rudy neighed from the far side of the corral.

"Don't tell me what to do," Aubrey said, stomping away.

Even though she'd put several feet between them, she heard his veiled threat clearly. "My ranch, my rules."

CHAPTER EIGHT

Dani sat down at her desk and opened a coloring book as Beck settled in his chair with more of a thump than usual. That woman would be the death of him. Not only did Aubrey disobey his orders, she knew exactly how to drive the knife into his back, though she'd didn't seem to realize it. He clenched his hands, trying to hold off the waves of guilt coursing through him.

What Aubrey had implied was true. He should have been there, with his sister, before she died. Should have known Dani before she'd gone silent. Maybe then he'd know how to break her free of this bubble of grief. It surprised Beck how much he wanted to see the child speak, laugh, squeal with joy.

God, how had he not known that Hope was that sick, how little time she had? He was such an idiot.

His niece picked up a blue crayon and colored the

toucan's body on the page, her face scrunched up as she worked to stay within the lines. Already she picked colors with a burgeoning artist's eye. Cassie's influence? He'd have to get her into some art classes after school started. Right now, there were more important things to focus on.

Glancing out the window, he saw Rudy at the fence, staring at the house. Another lost soul. He'd done everything possible for that horse, yet Rudy didn't want anything to do with him. Only her. Aubrey, with her long, straight hair the color of wheat, and eyes so expressive he saw the fire coming at him. Aubrey, with a runner's body, thin and lithe, yet curved in all the right places.

Drawn to her in a way he'd never been drawn to a woman before, Beck chided himself. The woman was trouble, but she was necessary for now. He still thought she should stay, because if she didn't, Beck was about out of options.

She'd stay. With her kind heart visible on her sleeve, she'd put up with anything to help that damn horse. And to help Dani.

Speaking of which ...

"Sweetie?"

Dani lifted her head, her eyes round and inquisitive.

Beck leaned down and took her free hand in his, turning it one way, then the other. So small compared to his. So smooth against his rough, work-worn skin.

"The woman, Aubrey?"

Dani's lips tipped downward.

"She might stick around for a while."

Dani shook her head, the movement growing as she got more agitated.

"Why don't you like her?"

Dani opened her mouth and Beck froze, sending prayers skyward that finally, Dani would talk.

She didn't. She closed her mouth again, speaking instead with the tears that dotted her face and the fear that widened her eyes.

"She helped you and your mother, didn't she?"

The vehement head shakes returned.

"She said she used to come over to the house and keep you both company. Isn't that true?"

The reluctance behind Dani's nod would have made Beck laugh if this conversation weren't so serious.

"She played with you, brought coloring books?"

Again, she nodded.

"But you don't like her?"

Head shake.

"Why not?"

Dani stared at him with desperation in her face.

"Is it because, um, she was there, uh, when your mommy went to heaven?"

The tears flowed now. Beck picked Dani up, cuddling her close as she cried. "Ah, honey, I'm so sorry. I'm sorry your mommy's not here. I'm sorry I wasn't there for her, and for you."

Silent tears became intermittent sniffles. Dani calmed, yet Beck felt no closer to understanding exactly why she'd taken such a dislike to Aubrey. He tried to picture that time in his mind, though it sliced his own wounds deeper. Hope, lying in a hospital bed in her home, Dani sitting beside her as they talked or colored. Aubrey visiting, bringing things for Dani and for Hope. Meds? No. She was a social worker. Paperwork? Orders for Hope to sign?

Aubrey would have been there more often as Hope's body lost its battle. She might have been there at the end. And now she was here. Could it be that simple?

"Sweetie, are you worried that Aubrey is here to help somebody else move to heaven?"

The sniffles increased, becoming wails as she clung to Beck. Cassidy poked her head in the door. When Beck held his hand up to show they were fine, she quietly closed the door behind her.

It was just Beck and Dani, awash in their sorrows. Beck held his niece tight. She'd never cried like this before that he'd seen. It had to be good for her, letting it out. Didn't it?

He whispered things to her, nothings he didn't even understand himself. Just his voice, wracked with grief, sharing with someone he loved.

Finally, when her sobs returned to the occasional sniffle, Beck reached for the Kleenex he now kept on his desk. Setting her up on his lap, he wiped her eyes and face with the same gentleness he used on newborn foals. Soothing strokes, light touches.

"I want to explain something to you," he said, keeping his voice quiet.

Dani looked at him with her large eyes.

"That woman, Aubrey? She didn't help your mother go to heaven."

Dani's lip trembled.

"She couldn't have. It wasn't her decision. God wanted your mommy to come help him watch over all his children. Aubrey ... well, she made it easier for your mother. For you. She helped you both."

Dani poked him in the chest several times.

"She's not here for me," Beck said, figuring it out. Except now, how to explain this to a six-year-old? "Look, sweetie, I can't promise I'll be around forever. None of us will. God loans us to this great land, and he'll want us all back at some point. But I'm not sick. No one here is sick. And Aubrey? I think she's as sorry your mommy's gone as we are."

He realized the truth of his words as he spoke them. That had to be the reason for the sadness in Aubrey's expression when he caught her unaware of his gaze.

"I think she came here to heal, just like you did. Just like I need to. And I think we should let her stay."

Dani didn't shake her head, didn't cry again. Hopefully, what Beck had said would help her understand.

"We also need her to help with Rudy. He likes her. She might help him find his happy place again."

Dani got down from Beck's lap and went to the window, staring at the horse who stared right back at her. Whatever connection lay between these two, it was strong. No, not two. Three. A triangle of contact between Dani, Rudy, and Aubrey that he wasn't privy to. He'd need to watch them all carefully to make sure none of them got hurt through this process.

"What do you think, sweetie? Should we let Aubrey stay?"

Dani kept her gaze forward out the window, but her nod of acceptance held no hesitation.

"Good. I'll tell her she can stay."

~~~

That man was the most infuriating, arrogant ... Aubrey paced the bedroom that, right now, felt like a prison.

"How can your brother be so much the opposite of you?" Aubrey asked, looking out the window toward the azure sky. She plopped onto the bed, hanging her head and giving in to futility and despair. Dani was afraid of her, Beck didn't want her there, and Rudy? The one living entity she had any chance of bonding with had been forbidden to her unless Beck was with her. Forbidden! No one had ordered Aubrey around in a long time, and she wasn't about to take it now. She needed a plan. Something that helped her, Dani, and the horse. And to hell with Beckett
~~~

Hawthorne.

What were her choices? She could leave or stay.

If she left, she wouldn't see Dani anymore, unless the social worker deemed Beck an unfit guardian. Aubrey had seen him with Dani. Despite that vile temper of his, he was nothing but gentle with the girl. Leaving the ranch also meant leaving Rudy. It surprised Aubrey how much the horse had come to mean to her.

She couldn't say goodbye to them. Not yet. She'd stay, but she'd be damned if she'd take orders from Beck. He needed to learn she had a mind of her own. She wanted time with Dani, so that must be her focus. To that end, she needed to understand how this ranch worked and what Dani's schedule was. An idea began to form in her mind, and before long, Aubrey had a plan. She left her room and went in search of Cassidy.

She found her still in the barn office. Aubrey knocked on the door jamb and waited for a "come in" before she entered.

"Hey, Cassie."

"Hi!" Cassie grinned like someone completely satisfied with life.

"Where's Dani?"

"She and Beck rode down to the mailbox."

Dani rides? Well, of course, Aubrey berated herself. This is a ranch. But she was only six. Wasn't she too young? "He doesn't put her on a horse by herself, does he?"

"They work with a pony he bought for her. But no, when they ride the ranch, he sets her in front of him on his horse."

"That makes sense. Are you, umm, busy?"

"There's always things need doing, but I've got time." She motioned to a chair in front of the desk.

Aubrey sank into the comfortable leather and looked

around at all the tack hanging on walls. "If you don't like horses, why do you work in the barn?"

Cassie laughed. "Well, for one thing, there isn't any more office space available in the house. All the bedrooms are being converted for the bed and breakfast. Plus, people have to come find me out here, so I get more done. And even though I don't care for horses, I grew up around this smell." She shrugged. "It's home."

"I think I can understand that. It's like Seattle traffic. I miss those sounds at night. It's so quiet here."

"That it is."

Uncertain how to proceed, Aubrey hesitated.

"You need help," Cassidy said. "Right?"

She nodded. "I never met Beck before yesterday. But I knew Dani."

Cassie sat back in her chair. "From the screaming I heard last night, and how tense she got today when you walked in, I get the impression Dani doesn't like you much."

Aubrey struggled to hold back tears. "I don't know why. I'd like to remedy that."

"How?"

"I'd hoped you might help me find ways to be around Dani. Maybe schooling her, if she got more comfortable around me. It would free you up for your other duties."

"First, how do you know Dani?"

"I was the hospice social worker assigned to Hope Hawthorne's case. We became friends."

"So you were there through the end."

"Yes." She barely breathed, afraid all the memories and grief might overwhelm her yet again.

Cassie nodded. "That explains a lot, including why you need some healing yourself."

Aubrey looked down, an errant tear plopping onto her

jeans.

"Grief is a tough process, but a necessary one."

Looking up into sympathetic eyes, Aubrey gave a little laugh. "Anyone ever tell you you're an old soul in a young body?"

"A few times. Better than a young soul in an old body."

They both laughed. Cassie pulled her chair closer to her desk, leaned her elbows on it, and rested her chin on her hands. She stared at Aubrey for a bit and Aubrey stared back, feeling like her own soul was being laid out for the girl to see.

"You're right," Cassie said, straightening. "Dani needs you around. And I know exactly how to make that happen."

This was the help Aubrey needed. A kindred spirit to carve the way to a better relationship with the little girl. "How?" She couldn't keep the excited tone out of her voice.

"Every weekday at two in the afternoon, Dani has her horse-riding lessons."

"I could watch them. Good idea."

"Do you ride?"

"Not in a long time. I'd be a horrible instructor."

"Oh, I'm not talking about you teaching Dani. You two should take lessons at the same time."

Aubrey had a sinking feeling she knew where this was headed.

Cassie grinned. "From Beck."

Shaking her head, Aubrey sank back into the cushions. "Not a good idea." Her gut churned just thinking of being in an arena with Beck, and not just because they were oil and vinegar.

"If Dani sees you faltering, being human, it will warm

her toward you. Then, if you can melt that fear of hers, I'd be happy to have you sit in with us at lessons while you're here. Maybe even take over if it works out." Cassie spread her arms. "It's all I've got."

What was it about ranch folk that they treated every decision like it was black or white? Everything had layers of gray, and there had to be some choices in the gray that didn't feature Beck as part of the equation. Except Aubrey didn't have a single alternate solution. For now, Cassie's suggestion would have to be it.

"Fine. I'll take lessons with Dani." She stood. "But I won't take any of his crap. I hope you understand."

"Maybe, maybe not. Remember," she said with an insufferably innocent smile, "Beck is Dani's lifeline. She won't look kindly on anyone who gets angry with him."

Aubrey chewed her lower lip to squash a retort. After some thought, she nodded. "Cassie, you're out to get me."

Cassie came around the desk and hugged Aubrey. "No. I'm on your side. Believe that. In fact, I'm on all of your sides. Now, do you have any boots?" She glanced down at the flips on Aubrey's feet.

"Nothing like what you've got on. I brought my hiking boots, though."

"Those will have to do. Your feet will swim in a pair of mine. Okay, be at the barn at 2 p.m. I'll ask Pops to saddle a horse up for you."

Aubrey walked back to the house feeling like she'd just been hoodwinked and she couldn't find a way around it. To get on Dani's good side, she'd have to deal with Beck.

She headed for the kitchen, needing fortitude before she took on that problem.

CHAPTER NINE

The arena, newly completed, smelled of fresh wood and satisfaction. Beck knew it would be an excellent place for showcasing his horses to prospective breeders. One half of the arena lay in shade, with the other half open to the sunshine and elements. He'd ordered large heaters to allow year-round use. For the moment, this was his niece's playground.

Beck settled Dani on Sam's back. The pony, steady and small, was perfect for daring little girls who had minds of their own. He stood patiently, even as Dani nudged his sides to get him moving. Having been purchased from a program that offered rides and lessons to the disabled, Sam waited for Beck's direction.

Each day at lesson time, Dani tugged on Beck until they were out the door and headed toward the stables. She did whatever she could with her little hands to help him saddle Sam, and she did it with more patience than he'd expect from a six-year-old. He didn't need words to understand her enthusiasm for horses. The sparkle in her eyes and wide smile on her face proved Dani was a born horse person. It made buying this ranch, and all the headaches that went with it, worth it.

Now, as she waited poised on her pony's back, Dani stiffened. Beck turned to see why and saw Aubrey standing at the entrance to the arena holding the reins of a chestnut named Sadie.

What the hell?

With a tight grip on Sam's halter, Beck walked to the gate, aware the entire time of how good she looked in her form-fitting jeans and a pink t-shirt that molded to her skin. She held the reins with ease. Did she know how to ride?

"What's this all about?" he asked, stopping inside the gate.

Aubrey shuffled from foot to foot. "Cassie didn't tell you?"

"Tell me what?"

"She suggested I join your lessons with Dani." Aubrey glanced at the girl, a tentative smile on her face. "She, umm, thought I could use a refresher course. It's been a while."

He needed to have a long conversation with Cassidy after he finished this lesson. "How long a while?"

Aubrey shrugged. "Ten years or so?"

"How much riding did you do?"

"Only the occasional girlfriend afternoon hangout ride. I took some lessons, though."

That explained her apparent ease standing next to Sadie. Horses intimidated newbies, especially when no fence stood between them.

"This won't work. I need to focus on Dani. I can't watch both of you." *And keep you safe.*

She looked at him, unwavering. "I agree Dani is your first consideration. I'm willing to stay on the sidelines while you work with her, soak some lessons up and refresh my memory."

He shook his head, mumbling. "What was Cassidy thinking?"

"I asked her the same thing. She said it would be good for all of us." Aubrey glanced again at Dani.

Oh, yes, Beck would definitely have a long talk with Cassidy. Today. He looked at Dani. She wasn't stiff any longer. Some of the light had gone from her eyes, but she didn't look afraid. Her reaction to Aubrey was more curious than anything else, and included a hint of longing that surprised him. Maybe their talk had helped. Beck liked the idea that Dani listened to him. It surprised him how much he'd grown to love this child, and that it had been immediate, from the first time he'd met her.

His attraction to Aubrey, the worst reminder of his gravest sin, complicated things. Was this part of his penance? Beck reached for the gate latch. "You stand beside your horse at the edge of the corral. You don't get on until I've checked out your ability. Got it?"

Aubrey saluted him with a straight face, then, grim-lipped, walked Sadie into the arena and stopped beside the fence.

Beck frowned, vowing to have that talk with Cassidy as soon as this lesson was over. At least Aubrey had done what she was told. *That's once.*

While not thrilled at having this audience, Beck put Dani and Sam through their usual paces. For a six-year-old, she had an uncanny knack for understanding her mount. If she wasn't so tiny, he'd get her a small horse. Beck wasn't ready to put her higher off the ground. Not yet. For now, he'd let her hone her skills on stalwart Sam. He smiled as she roamed the arena, ranging farther and farther away from him, barely using the reins. Sam understood her leg nudges, turning this way and that upon command.

Beck got so wrapped up in Dani, jogging beside her and the pony, that he forgot about Aubrey. By the time he ended the lesson, both he and the girl sported wide grins. He lifted Dani off the horse and twirled her around in the air. Her peal of laughter soothed his soul better than anything.

"You did good, sweetie. Really good. You're a natural." He set her down. She patted Sam, reached for the reins, then her uncle's hand. Together, they walked to the gate and opened it. Mack, one of the ranch hands, took Sam's reins from Dani. Beck was about to leave with his niece when he remembered Aubrey standing there next to Sadie, waiting.

"Let Sam pasture," he told Mack, then he looked down at Dani. "I'll work with Aubrey now. You can watch from outside the fence, or you can go find Cassidy."

Dani climbed the fence, holding on tight, giving Beck his answer. She was staying put.

He walked over to Aubrey and the horse, surprised to see tears in her eyes. Beck cocked his head. When she smiled to show him the tears were happy ones, the corners of his own lips lifted.

"That was amazing to watch, Beck. You love working with horses, don't you?" she said, wiping her eyes.

Beck nodded. He did. He understood them. Well, most of them. He refused to look behind him where he was certain Rudy stood watching from the corral across the driveway.

"And you really love Dani."

"Of course, I do."

"So do I," she whispered. "So much. I ... I loved

watching you two out there. Th-thank you."

What the—? Beck could handle stubborn Aubrey. Even angry Aubrey. But this version? It tore at his heartstrings. He wanted to cocoon her, let her be part of what he shared with the horses, with Dani. He wanted to draw her into his arms and open his world to her. Her eyes were so expressive. Wide when angry or surprised, all crinkled up and almost disappearing when she smiled, then tender, open, and vulnerable when sad.

He almost reached for her, barely holding himself back. He cleared his throat, patted Sadie. "Amos picked a good horse for you. Sadie's neither docile nor full of vinegar, but somewhere in between."

"Amos is Cassie's father, right?"

Beck nodded, feeling much surer on this ground. "And my right-hand man. He's got more ranch know-how than I'll ever have. I couldn't run this place without him. All right, let's find out where you are with your riding."

Aubrey nodded, tugging at the ponytail fed through the back of the ball-cap she wore. She turned toward Sadie. The horse wasn't the biggest Beck owned, yet Aubrey's diminutive height meant she'd need a stool to get on Sadie's back.

"I'll help you mount."

"Thanks. Being short has its drawbacks."

Beck wove his fingers together and stooped while she placed her boot in his grasp.

"Ready?"

"Yes."

Light as she was, he lifted her easily. Their hands touched when they both reached for the horn. The feel of her soft skin on his ignited something inside Beck. Aubrey's eyes widened, becoming dark pools. Her mouth, shaped in that "o" of surprise, looked so kissable Beck almost pulled her down to do just that.

With a stern mental shake, he handed her Sadie's reins. She settled in the saddle well, which indicated the experience she'd mentioned was real. Still, he stayed. Being close felt good, felt right, and he wanted more of it.

He straightened and backed up a couple steps. She sat like a natural, straight-backed but at ease, holding the reins with just enough tension.

She looked good. Too good.

"Well, you know how to sit a horse," he said, his tone gruffer than he'd planned.

Squinting at him, Aubrey said nothing.

"Walk the perimeter. Let me see how you and Sadie do together."

Beck stayed put as she nudged the horse with a gentle knee, using a bare touch on the reins. Good instincts.

After she'd walked the arena, he suggested a trot. He could see her struggle to sit the new rhythm, and smiled when she figured it out on her own.

After a couple rounds, he motioned her over.

The wide smile on her face radiated happiness, but he asked anyway. "How's it feel?"

"Amazing. I can't believe I waited so long to do this."

"Okay. Ready to try a canter? How about some figure eights?"

"Definitely." She headed out without direction, working Sadie into the pattern, then nudging her to a canter. She rode better than he expected, and she looked hot doing it. Beck's grin widened when he glanced at Dani and saw her smiling, too.

He let Aubrey do a few more figure eights before calling an end to this first session. She pulled up beside him, her face aglow with pleasure. Beck walked around the horse as she swung a leg over the horn. He grabbed her by the waist to help her dismount, again struck by some foreign emotion that wrapped itself around him. What was it about being close to this woman that enticed him so? She smelled of sunshine and flowers, and the vulnerability in her eyes brought out every protective instinct inside him. He kept his hands at her waist when he wanted to do so much more. Beck dropped his gaze to lips that parted, inviting him in, and he leaned down, ready to claim them.

Until he heard Dani scuffling her way down the fence, righting his world. He did not have time for any relationship except the one with his niece, and something told him Aubrey wasn't the one-off, casual hookup kind.

Straightening, he reached for the reins. "A good first lesson. Won't be long before you'll be ready for a ride out on the ranch."

Aubrey rubbed her butt cheek and Beck bit back a groan.

"I think I'll be sore, but the only way to get over it is to keep doing it, right?"

"That and a long, hot soak." That was a visual he didn't need, either. Damn, had it been that long? All of a sudden, he couldn't think about anything but her, like some rutting stag. This had to stop.

"Well, thank you." Aubrey held out her hand, hesitated as if she wished she hadn't done it, then thrust it out further. "I appreciate the chance."

Beck took her hand, holding it longer than necessary. "Tomorrow, then."

"Yes, umm, tomorrow."

Beck let her hand go and reached for Sadie's reins, then walked to the gate where Dani stood waiting. Once they were through, Aubrey closed and latched the arena gate, then glanced at Dani, whose smile disappeared when Aubrey got closer. Aubrey's eyes got misty, but she didn't push it with the girl. She squatted down in place, not moving any closer.

"Thanks for loaning me your uncle so I could do some riding. I enjoyed that a lot. I bet you did, too. Except, I think I'll be sore."

Dani's frown lightened and a shade of compassion touched her eyes.

"I can take Sadie back to the barn," Aubrey told Beck, standing. "I'd like to brush her down. I always enjoyed doing that after rides."

"All right. Amos can help you find what you need. That frees me up to get on to kitchen duty."

He stood there with Dani as Aubrey and the horse walked away, unable to stop appreciating the sway of her hips in those jeans. Shaking his head, he held his hand out to Dani. "Time to get grub going for the crew."

Regretfully, he turned and headed to the house, Dani's hand in his.

Something had changed today. He wasn't sure what, and was even less sure he liked it. But somehow, Aubrey had turned into something more than a burden. His interest in her had taken a turn, become something more.

He was so screwed.

~~~

Aubrey's hand shook as she brushed Sadie. It took several passes before she calmed enough to even out her strokes. Sadie nickered.

"Sorry, girl." Aubrey lightened her strokes. "Relearning this." And trying to calm down. What the heck had happened out there? The attraction between her and Beck had caught Aubrey off guard. At one point, she'd been sure he was about to kiss her. And she'd wanted him to. That first touch had stirred a longing inside her she didn't even know she could feel. His eyes, when he wasn't frowning,
~~~

were kind. Yet sometimes, when he looked at her, they grew intense and dark.

She didn't need this. Didn't want to be attracted to Beck.

"I can't do this," she said, talking to the horse. "I can't like him. I can't. I'm not in my right mind," she muttered. "It's just my heart searching for relief from the pain. That's what it has to be. A grief reaction, like a rebound relationship."

Sadie cocked her head and stared at Aubrey with one eye.

"Don't look at me like that. It's a real thing. Or, at least, it should be."

Aubrey finished brushing Sadie, gave her a carrot, and closed the stall door behind her, still unclear if there was a solution to her problem. She stared at the brush, then deciding on the perfect distraction, she headed for the forbidden corral. This time, she walked to the back side of the fence where prying eyes in the house wouldn't find her, at least not without effort. Rudy followed her and stood docile as she climbed over the fence. His shiver as she touched his forehead made her want to cry.

"What happened to you?" Aubrey leaned against him, not caring that Rudy's neck was caked with mud. She placed her hand alongside his cheek, staying still and silent until his tremors subsided. "What made you so afraid?" She wondered if she really wanted to know.

She stepped back and looked at the patches of brown and white. Well, she thought he had some white under all that mud.

"Hey, boy, I've got something for you." She pulled the carrot out of her back pocket and held her hand flat, offering the treat. Rudy took it without hesitation. Next, Aubrey held the curry comb out for Rudy to get a good look at. He sniffed it warily, but only trembled for a moment as she touched it to his neck.

"You trust me, don't you, boy?" Keeping her voice soft and her strokes light, she talked to Rudy as she brushed the caked-on mud from him. He needed a hose bath, but this would do for now.

In careful, circular motions, she brushed off the dry dirt, watching for any adverse reaction. Hope had liked horses. She used to have one, though she'd sold it before Aubrey met her, one of the few things that had made Hope sad. Aubrey, who'd spent a little time around horses, understood. These animals could be kindred spirits. She thought of Beck and Rudy and smiled. Or thorns in your side.

"You watched me ride Sadie a while ago. I hope you weren't jealous. She's a good horse, and I needed to remember how to ride. You understand that, don't you, boy?"

Rudy turned an eye toward her and Aubrey smiled at him as she continued to brush. "You'd have loved Hope. She loved to ride. Said it reminded her of her childhood." Aubrey glanced around. "In fact, she'd love this place. Oh, gosh, she did love this ranch. That's right. She lived here." Aubrey gazed around with a new appreciation for the place Mara had sent her. Hope Ranch.

A hawk cried overhead, searching for food. Aubrey watched it soar, finding solace, rare these days, in the raptor's glide. She rested her hand on Rudy's neck and watched. Life went on, no matter what.

Had Beck seen the hawk? Did he ever take time to look up, to see the extraordinary world that surrounded him? A vision wafted through her brain like a happy song. Her, Beck, and Dani sat on that big front porch. Then, as the day waned, Beck stood and held out his hand to

Aubrey. He pulled her up and, after a kiss filled with promise, they swung Dani between them while they strolled for a visit with Rudy.

The horse huffed, startling Aubrey from her reverie. She straightened and went back to brushing him, her good mood fading as she tried to make sense of her attraction to Beck. She should hate him. She needed to hate him. Liking him meant being unfaithful to Hope's memory. Beck never once visited his sister, not even at the end. Nothing excused that, no matter the why. His absence had caused Hope pain and Aubrey found that unconscionable.

He also had way too many authoritarian genes in his makeup, telling her what to do, giving her orders. Yet, when she'd been astride Sadie, he'd been gentle and complimentary. Plus, he looked so damn good in jeans and a t-shirt, tipping his black cowboy hat back on his head to wipe sweat from his brow, smiling when she did something good, his eyes crinkling up.

But what struck her the most was the way he looked at Dani, with eyes full of love, tinged with more than a little worry. He cared for her and would do whatever was necessary to ensure Dani's happiness.

A complicated man, that's what Beck Hawthorne was. She vowed to steer clear of him. They had the same goals where Dani was concerned, but that was all they had in common.

Aubrey brushed back toward Rudy's flank and he skittered away. She moved with him, soothing him with her hands and voice, but the tremors returned. Aubrey held the brush so Rudy could smell it again. She set it on the ground and ran her hand along his hip. Ridges, raised lines that weren't natural, lay there. Several of them. And Rudy's shaking had increased.

Whip marks. That's what they were. Aubrey's

trembling hand flew to her mouth as tears stung her eyes. Rudy had been whipped, and hard enough to leave scars. She hung her head, resting her hands on the horse, trying to understand how someone could do something like this to such a beautiful animal, to any animal. How could this happen? Aubrey clenched her hands, needing something to throw, some way to vent her anger at whoever had done this. Until she noticed Rudy shivering. She reached for him, but he side-stepped, sensing her ire. It took everything Aubrey had, along with a few deep breaths, to calm herself. Speaking quiet nothings, Aubrey stepped back to Rudy's head, brushing her hand along his neck. Soothing strokes, with a voice to match, though her insides were in turmoil.

"Someone hurt you, didn't they? Shame on them. You're too nice a guy to be treated that way. I get it. I understand your reticence now. And we've made good strides, you and me."

Slowly, the fear left his eyes and he relaxed. Only then did Aubrey pick up the curry comb and move to the other side, brushing his neck until Rudy relaxed. The shade didn't hide the faint whip scars at his hip on that side, too.

"Don't worry. I won't go there. I'll just brush here and along your flank. We'll work on those hips another day."

Someone had beaten Rudy, that much was certain. Aubrey finished brushing him and offered her last carrot, still wondering about the marks. Did Beck know about them? Had he thought to have a vet look at Rudy? To try to clean him up, just a little? Those scars weren't recent, and Aubrey found it hard to believe Beck would harm any horse. Though now, a couple burning questions filled her with unease.

How long had Beck owned Rudy and why wasn't he, or anyone at the ranch, trying to make Rudy's life better?

CHAPTER TEN

After dinner, Beck started the dishwasher, then grabbed a beer from the fridge and headed out to join his ranch family around their twice-weekly campfire. It had been a long, hard work week for everyone, and it had been worth it. Next week, the man he hoped would sell him his first breeding stock would visit. They were ready, so now it was time for everyone to relax.

He saw Aubrey settled next to Cassidy on a log. The two were having an animated conversation about something. He leaned against the corner of the house and watched. Aubrey's arms were all over the place as she made her point. He smiled at how hard she was working to convince Cassidy of something.

Everyone sat in pairs, threes, or alone. All with their beverage of choice, all content to enjoy the evening after a hard day's work. Dani sat as far away from Aubrey as possible, next to Amos. Beck wandered around, slapping shoulders, thanking them, and checking in to be sure each one was in a good place.

"All good here," Amos said.

Beck sat down in a chair next to him and pulled Dani onto his lap. Unable to stop himself, he glanced at Aubrey, whose effervescence died out as she frowned back at him. Why was she frowning?

"What do you think?" Amos said.

"I'm sorry, what?"

Amos snorted. "You are in deep."

"I don't know what you're talking about," Beck said, though he had a pretty good idea what his friend's statement was about. Or rather, who.

"Ooh, in denial, huh? Well, it'll get you in the end. Just like it got me." Amos' grin faded. "Been five years and I still miss her."

Beck gripped his shoulder in support. "It can't be easy."

Amos, his parent's ranch manager, had joined Beck on this adventure before the ink had dried on the contract to buy the place. Beck was grateful to have him there. He'd filled all the holes and knew a good sight more about ranching than Beck. That was why, from the beginning, Beck's arrangement with Amos included living quarters and, when they made a profit, a percentage of the take. The man was earning it. Beck had hoped it would ease his friend's loneliness. Yvonne, his wife and Cassidy's mother, had passed away from cancer long before they'd reconnected, but the grief was still evident in Amos' face.

He knew that feeling. "Does it ever get easier?" he asked quietly, giving Dani a hug.

"Easier?" Amos shook his head. "No. Gets tolerable. That's all. You'll feel better in time, son. That's the only fix, and it's not a complete one."

Beck nodded and they stared into the fire, full of their own thoughts. When Beck looked up, it was into Aubrey's soulful blue eyes. She seemed to see right through his disguise, right into the core of his pain. Even as he was attracted to her, it hurt to be near her. To know she'd been there when he hadn't.

He looked away, raking a hand through his hair. God, would he ever get past this? Full of nervous energy, he stood, setting Dani down in his chair. He threw another log on the fire.

"Hey, boss," Cassidy said, joining him. "Want me to put Dani to bed?"

"That would be great." Beck picked Dani up and gave her a hug. He touched his finger to her nose. "'Night, sweetie."

Dani touched her finger to his nose and gave him a sticky kiss on his cheek.

"Tootsie pop?" he asked Cassidy.

"Yep. Sorry."

Beck waved his hand in dismissal. "A sign that she had a sticky, good time."

Dani walked off with Cassidy. When she glanced at Aubrey, Beck saw the flash of apprehension in her face. He thought he'd reassured her, but it seemed this was one more thing it would take her time to get past.

"Well, morning comes early," Amos said. "Think I'll follow suit."

"'Night," Beck said, watching the man walk off, his shoulders bowed. Was love worth that kind of pain? He thought of Hope. For the first time, good memories overrode the bad. Hope, helping him build a hay-bale fort. Making cow-pie cookies, then trying to feed them to the cows. Hope, sneaking out at night to sleep with her favorite horse. Much like her daughter.

Did Aubrey know that Hope? She'd want to. Beck was certain of that. Was he ready to tell the stories? That's where Beck's certainty ended, and the only way to know for sure was to try.

With a deep breath, he walked over and sat in the spot Cassidy had vacated. "How was the rest of your day?"

"Fine," Aubrey answered, monotone.

"What did you do?"

"What is this, an inquisition?"

Where the hell was this coming from? She sounded angry and they hadn't been inside the same fence for hours. God help him, even when the woman exasperated him, he loved that fire in her eyes.

Beck frowned. "What did I do that has you so ticked off?"

"Pretty arrogant to think it's you I'm angry with."

Beck held up two hands. "Five minutes ago, you were laughing with Cassidy. Besides, who else have you had time to get pissed off at?"

"True."

"Excuse me?"

"All right." Aubrey turned to face Beck, the full force of her ire almost making him back up. "How long have you owned Rudy?"

The question surprised him. "Not long. A friend of mine asked me to take him on, try to bring him around."

Seconds ticked by as Aubrey searched his face. Where was this headed?

"He has whip marks."

Whip marks? Yes, the horse did. Beck knew all about them, but Aubrey didn't. Wait a minute— "You went into the corral, didn't you? Against my express wishes. And, if you saw those welts on his haunches, you got up close and personal. Again, very much against my instructions."

At least she had the decency to look chagrined, though it was fleeting. Her Anger quickly returned. "You can't order me around."

"On my ranch, I can. Don't you get it? It's for your own safety."

"I can take care of myself."

"My ranch, my rules. Remember?"

"Well, your rules are stupid."

"And I didn't whip that damn horse, if that's what you're really trying to ask."

Beck sat back and took a deep breath, trying to calm the building rage within him. He looked around at the same time Aubrey did, as surprised as she seemed to be to find the campfire devoid of people. Somehow, in only a minute or two, everyone had cleared out. Beck had never seen that happen before.

"So you really didn't whip Rudy?"

"What the hell do you think of me, that you'd think I would injure a horse like that?" Beck tried and failed to keep his voice down. "I rescued him. Well, not me, exactly. Someone else did, then they reached out to me, asking if I'd take him on and help heal his wounds. Except I haven't been able to. Damn horse won't let me near him."

The quick hit of guilt on Aubrey's face surprised him. Giving him no chance to consider it, she fired her next question.

"How long has he been here?"

"Two weeks before you arrived, and he looks as mangy now as he did then because we can't get near him. They had to tranq him to get him in the trailer. Horse was out of his mind with fear. Even sedated, he broke a man's hand, crushing it against the wall. The vet had to look him over from afar, and I'm the only one that feeds him. I won't let any more of my men get hurt by that horse. That's why I don't want you near him. He's dangerous."

"He's not dangerous to me."

Beck sighed. This impasse between them would not go away. "Let me rephrase this in a more palatable way, then. Please stay away from Rudy unless I'm with you." He let some of his fear for her show. "I have enough on my hands with an emotionally wounded horse and a child who won't speak, even though she can. I don't need another injured person."

Aubrey held his gaze, stripping everything away until there was nothing left but raw emotion. When Aubrey's hand settled on his arm, Beck broke eye contact. He stared at her long fingers, like a pianist's. Did she play? He couldn't help himself. He reached for her hand, pulling it into his. It felt good there. It felt right, having her beside him. He rubbed his thumb across delicate knuckles. Her skin was so smooth against his ranch-hardened hands.

Her mouth, with that full lower lip, beckoned him as much as her eyes, still focused on him. On his lips.

Beck bent his head and moved toward her.

Aubrey leaned in.

Their lips touched, sending a ripple through him he didn't understand. He clutched her hand while the other slipped around her neck, pulling her in tighter.

She didn't resist.

Gentle became urgent. Beck reached out with his tongue and Aubrey opened to him, met him with her own. He threaded his hand through her hair, wanting to never let her go, to keep this going, keep everything else at bay.

Except Aubrey wasn't meant to be some stop-gap between him and his guilt. She was better than that.

With reluctance, he broke the kiss. They sat there, forehead to forehead, each working to catch their breath.

When Beck pulled away, pools of emotion followed

him. Her lips ... Oh, God, her lips were swollen and red from their kiss.

"That shouldn't have happened," he said, his voice gruffer than he'd planned.

He caught a glimpse of the hurt caused by his words before she managed to hide it. He was such a heel.

"I guess it shouldn't have." Aubrey stood, smoothing her hands down her jeans. "I'd better get to bed."

Exactly where he wanted her. Laid out, her hair fanned, her face flush with desire as her eyes begged him to join her. Beck shook his head.

"Yes, well, I'll check on Rudy, then hit the hay myself."

"Mind if I go along?"

Even with the fire dying down, he could see her blush.

"I mean, to check on Rudy."

He didn't want to be anywhere near her right now. He wanted to take a cold shower and drive all thoughts of Aubrey from his mind, his groin, his heart. "Sure."

They walked together, though several feet separated them. At the corral, they searched for Rudy, barely seeing him on the far side of the corral, lying down, though not on his side. Beck squinted. There was something with him. Something small and light-colored.

Dani!

Before Beck raced in, Aubrey stopped him with surprising strength.

"You can't go get her."

"I have to. That horse will kill her."

"Look at them. They're relaxed. If you rush in there, you'll spook Rudy and that's when you run the real risk of Dani being hurt."

"What the hell do you expect me to do?"

"Let me go."

Beck shook his head. "No way."

"Please." Aubrey turned his face to hers. "I was in the corral today. I brushed Rudy. He's gentle with me. Not scared. It's the same with Dani. I'm the best chance you have of getting Dani out of there unharmed."

Beck ground his teeth. He didn't like it, but she was right, damn it. He gave a quick, hard nod, and Aubrey opened the gate and walked into the corral. Fear constricted Beck's breathing as he watched. If anything happened to Dani, or to her ...

"Hey, boy," Aubrey said as she walked with slow precision toward the horse and girl. "I see you've got a friend there. Good for you. Dani, your uncle wants you to come out of the corral now. I'm going to pet Rudy, to make sure he stays calm."

Beck couldn't tell if Dani listened to her or not. Damn it, there just wasn't enough light. And this was taking too long.

"Come on, honey. I'm here to walk you out to Beck."

Did Dani just shake her head?

"You and Rudy have a special relationship, don't you? So do you and your uncle. And right now he's pretty worried. He'd like to see that you're all right. Are you all right?"

Some movement occurred, but nothing decipherable. Beck unlatched the gate and forced himself to wait.

Aubrey was beside the horse now, crouching down. Beck squinted. Did the horse just push his nose into her hand, begging for attention? The same horse that about bit his off when he tried the same thing?

"Rudy, it's time for Dani to go to bed now. I know you understand. I'll be back in the morning, and Dani will be around the ranch. For tonight, she needs to sleep in her own bed."

Aubrey held out her hand to Dani and Beck held his

breath for an eternity, waiting for Dani to react, praying she'd take Aubrey's hand.

When she did, he blew out his pent up breath. Aubrey stood and she and Dani walked hand-in-hand until they were beyond the gate. Beck closed it, resisting the desire to slam it shut, and pulled Dani into his arms. He dug his face into her neck, breathing in her sweet essence. "Oh, God, Dani, if anything happened to you, I don't know what I'd do."

Beck pulled back, surprised to see tears on Dani's face. Because of him?

Aubrey saw them, too. She put a hand on Beck's back, urging them toward the house.

Inside, he turned to her and mouthed a "thank you" before heading upstairs with Dani. At the top, he turned again. Aubrey stood there with such love on her face for Dani it almost hurt him to see it.

He crawled into bed with his niece and stayed there long after she fell asleep, trying to come to terms with the plethora of emotions that raged through him. Abject fear, guilt, grief.

"Hope, what the hell were you thinking, giving this child to me? I love her like my own, but I'm so afraid. For her. For me. Ah, Sis, I'm so sorry I didn't understand how bad things were." His own tears fell on Dani's head as she slept, but sleep eluded Beck until well into the night.

~~~

Aubrey woke up, or tried to. With one eye open, she glanced at her phone. Six in the morning. The front door slammed, then boots clomped down the steps. Life on a ranch began early.

Rolling onto her back, Aubrey stretched, arms overhead, and pointed her toes. Ouch! She bit her tongue to not cry out in pain. Her thighs and butt were on fire. Oh,
~~~

Lordy. This riding thing wasn't for sissies, at least not when it was new again.

With care, she sat up, tested one leg, then stood and wobbled to the window, rubbing her sore behind. She wouldn't be doing much moving around today. A nice, long soak sounded much nicer.

Cassidy, well on her way to the barn, had a skip in her step. Aubrey smiled. That girl was perennially happy. Had that clomping boot step she'd heard moments ago come from her? No one else was around except Rudy, who leaned his head over the fence as if waiting for someone. Her or Dani? Or both? Last night, once she'd gotten beside the horse and his small friend and seen they were safe, her worry over the profound sadness in his eyes kept her up a good part of the night. At least, that's what she'd told herself. Her sleeplessness had nothing to do with one tall, stern, dark-eyed man in a cowboy hat. A man whose kiss had turned her world upside down. Once his lips touched hers, everything else had faded except him and the here-and-now. His lips on hers. Sparks racing through her body, ripples of electricity from lips both gentle and demanding. She wanted more. Oh, God, did she want more.

"I'm so sorry, Hope." Aubrey whispered the words. "I don't understand how this happened. He was horrible to you, yet I can't stay away from him. I want to be around him. What am I going to do?"

Rudy looked up at her window. Dani was as drawn to this horse as she was. Maybe that was how to get through to Dani. Could Rudy help her and help himself at the same time?

Aubrey's gut told her Rudy was the knot at the end of the lifeline she and Dani were clinging to. Beck, too, it seemed. That horse was the only thing keeping them from falling apart. If they could mend his heart, heal at least some of his pain, maybe they'd all find a way to be happy again.

A slight breeze blew in the open window, lifting the curtains. Aubrey smiled. Had Hope just approved? Whether she had or not, it was the only plan Aubrey had. She reached for her clothes and headed downstairs, no easy task considering her soreness.

Beck turned around when she entered the kitchen, his perennial scowl firmly in place when he saw her disjointed steps.

"You did too much yesterday." He turned back to the scrambled eggs.

"I figured that out."

"Take it easy today."

"No."

His head whipped around. "What?"

"I said no. I need to work with Rudy."

"Absolutely not."

"Well, I say absolutely yes."

She leaned against the fridge and watched his jaw shift from side to side.

"I have a ranch to run. I can't spend all day keeping you safe from some deranged horse."

"He's not deranged. He's in pain."

"Those scars have healed."

"Not the ones inside." Aubrey crossed her arms over her chest. Beck glanced down, his jaw grinding again.

"Your eggs are burning."

He got back to stirring. "Your eggs, you mean. The rest of us have eaten and are going on about our ranch business."

He'd stayed behind to make certain she had something to eat? Aubrey's re-hardened heart re-melted a little. "Thank you. You didn't have to do that."

"Needed to make sure you had some food."

Aubrey almost smiled at the gruff tone of his voice. "I can cook, you know."

"I didn't know, but now that I do, I'll let you take care of yourself. Breakfast is at 5am here. You're welcome to join us. Anything later, you're on your own."

She stifled the strong desire to salute. "Got it."

He gave a clipped nod in response, dished her eggs onto a plate, added bacon and a pancaked hash-brown potato. Setting it on the kitchen table, he grabbed a glass of orange juice from the fridge and placed it next to the plate. He pointed. "Breakfast."

"Again, thank you." Aubrey went to sit down, but with Beck so close, it seemed only natural to look up first. He would gnash that jaw into pulp if he kept working it that hard. She reached up and touched it, liking his stubble. His jaw relaxed, his eyes focused on her. It was just the two of them, here in this kitchen, staring at each other, trying to decipher whatever was happening between them.

A door slammed, breaking the moment. Beck stepped away, and Aubrey glanced down, letting her hair fall over her flaming face as she sank to a chair. What had she just done? All her resolve to bury her attraction to Beck had fled through the nearest open window.

She picked up her fork and toyed with her eggs. Beck set a cup of coffee next to the glass of juice.

"There's more in the pot. Help yourself."

"Thank you."

He walked around the table and toward the door.

"Beck?"

He froze.

"I need to work with Rudy. I'm not talking about riding him." Not today. "But I want to brush him again, see if he'll let me. Try to bond with him. It's important."

He didn't turn around. Straightening his shoulders, he let out a deep breath. "Fine. I'll meet you there in one hour." He turned to her. "Absolutely no riding."

Aubrey held up her hands. "Absolutely."

Beck shook his head and continued on to the door, but Aubrey wasn't finished.

"Beck?"

He stopped again, his shoulders rising as he took a breath. "What?"

Aubrey waited a beat. "I know you'd never hurt Rudy."

For long moments, Beck stood where he was, his back to her, then he strode out of the kitchen, leaving Aubrey feeling like she'd just won a very big battle.

CHAPTER ELEVEN

An hour later, Beck strode toward Rudy's corral, still unable to kill the irritation that roared through his ears like a hyena's scream. What was wrong with him? He had a day overfull with tasks and didn't have time to keep a horse from maiming a guest, but Aubrey would go ahead with or without him. He'd learned that the hard way. If he were being honest, he wanted to be around her, be near her. When they were together, his pain diminished. His heart felt lighter.

And that scared him more than anything. He must never forget. He wouldn't. That was his penance. To remember each day how badly he'd hurt his dying sister. Beck hung his head for a moment, the weight settling deeper on his shoulders.

He turned the corner of the house to see Aubrey watching him. She always did that. Watched him. It was infuriating. At least this time, she'd done it from the correct side of the fence. She hadn't tried to go into the corral without him.

Aubrey waited in those damn tight-fitting jeans and an open pastel plaid shirt over a white tank.

"Awfully clean clothes for the work you're wanting to do."

"You have a washing machine, right?"

He'd have thought nothing of it, except that she blushed a bright shade of red. "Dressed up for me, did you?"

"Not on your life." Her quick pivot belied the truth of that statement and Beck's mood lightened considerably as he opened the gate. He stepped in with her. "You can't come with me," she said.

"I get that. I spook Rudy, though I don't know why. I'll stand here, on the opposite side of the corral. Ready if anything happens."

She didn't like the idea. Tough.

"It's my way or not at all."

"Fine." She rolled her eyes.

He glanced inside the buckets she carried. Aubrey must have spoken to Amos or one of the hands. She had a curry comb and several brushes in the bucket. The other held water and a rag. She walked toward Rudy with slow confidence, the perfect attitude to have with a horse. Show them fear and they'll react accordingly. Rudy reacted on instinct, so fear or anger would set him off.

Beck leaned back against the fence rail to keep an eye on her.

Aubrey set the buckets down a ways from the wary horse. She picked up the curry comb first, holding it out for Rudy to sniff.

"You remember this, don't you, boy?"

The horse shivered, but he didn't shy away. Beck

watched as she combed him. She brushed like a natural. Small, circular motions to break loose the clumps of dirt, talking to Rudy the whole time in that throaty low voice of hers. Some of the words didn't make it to Beck, but Rudy paid attention. His ears were forward and his stance relaxed, though watchful. She worked her way across his flank, stopping before she got to the scars, moving to his other side. When she finished, she picked up the stiff-bristle brush and, after letting him sniff it, worked those same areas.

Something she said must have gotten Rudy's attention because he turned to stare at her. She laughed and the sound floated over to Beck like a happy sigh. Again, she stopped before getting to the scars. Back at the bucket, she grabbed the soft-bristled brush and showed it to the horse, just as she had with the others. This one, though, she ran her hands over, the bristles bending easily beneath her fingers. She brushed it along her skin where she'd rolled up her sleeves, then she brushed it along Rudy's nose. He never shivered or faltered. This horse had definitely picked his owner. Beck had to admire how well Aubrey handled him.

Brushing him the same as before, this time she didn't stop before the scars. She ran the brush over them. Just once, staying put with the brush on the horse's skin. Beck stiffened when he saw Rudy's head come up. Rudy turned his head and looked at Aubrey.

"Shh, shh, it's all right."

The world had gone so quiet, Beck heard her words clearly across the corral.

"I know someone hurt you. I won't do that and I think you know that. I only want to get some of this dirt off you. If we don't, these scars could get infected. Boy, would I like to get my hands on whoever did this to you." She kept her voice low and melodic, though Beck could hear the rise of emotion in her cadence.

Rudy watched her but didn't flinch as she brushed his haunch. First, she finished one side, then walked around the front of him to do the other. The horse let her do it.

The damn horse tolerated it. Beck shook his head and leaned back again, trying to figure out why Rudy let Aubrey get so close, yet Beck wasn't allowed within twenty feet. He'd done nothing to this horse except try to help him. It bothered him.

Aubrey crouched down. She planned to brush Rudy's legs.

"Not the legs," Beck said. "Too touchy."

"No, they're not. See?" She brushed along the foreleg with the soft bristles.

"Look at his ears."

She sat back and looked up. "Okay, they're turned back. He's not as comfortable with this. But he's not fighting me. He's not shivering, or kicking, or running. And they're caked in mud."

"He might kick at any moment. Leave the legs for another day."

"Darn, and I was going to dig out his hooves today, too."

"Funny." He'd made sure there was no hoof pick in her bucket, or a mane comb. All he needed was her standing at the business end of an unpredictable horse.

Thankfully, she didn't argue with him, heading back to the bucket instead. She wrung out the cloth. Back at the horse's side, Aubrey worked on his forehead and muzzle. Rudy stood quiet, ears forward and one leg bent, relaxed. Beck had to admit, the horse was taking it well, and the credit was all Aubrey's. She learned quickly and had a good head on her shoulders. Everything below was pretty nice as well. Too nice for his comfort.

He heard the tiny boots well before he felt the tug on his shirt. Dani climbed up and hung over the top rail of the fence.

"She's good, isn't she?"

Dani nodded.

"Rudy seems to like her."

Another nod.

"You like Rudy a lot. You okay with her being in there?"

Dani's face scrunched into a frown, but in a moment or two her serious expression eased and she smiled.

"So you don't think she's here for the reason you first thought?"

Her smile dipped when worry replaced satisfaction. But she only shrugged her shoulders. No vehement shaking, no tears. A clear improvement.

Or so he thought, until Dani stiffened. He'd let his guard down and turned away. Beck whipped around, but nothing had changed except that Aubrey smiled over at them. So Dani wasn't quite comfortable with their guest yet.

"You okay here?" Beck asked Dani. "I want to step closer to Rudy."

The vehement head shaking started.

"I'm not going to hurt him."

Dani pointed at the horse, then at Beck.

"You think he'll hurt me?"

Her stare was so forthright, so full of serious, he didn't have the heart to joke with her. Instead, he hugged her. "I'll be right back. I just need to see where things are with him and me."

Dani clutched the rail even tighter, but nodded.

Aubrey had finished and bent to put her brushes back

in the bucket, so she didn't notice him approaching.

Rudy did, however. His ears flattened and he huffed out a breath, his head jerking up. Aubrey looked up at him, still not seeing Beck until he spoke. "Aubrey?"

She stood so fast, she almost fell over.

Beck froze. "That horse is going mean again."

"Then stay where you are, Beck. Please, for all that's sacred in your life, let me deal with Rudy until we find a way for him to warm up to you. Please." She'd placed a hand on Rudy's neck and the horse turned an eye to her. His ears turned toward her, away from Beck.

"See, Beck? He's good with me. Give him time to adapt. Today is a big step for him."

He didn't like it, but she was right. "Fine. But time's up. I've got other things to get to, including lessons this afternoon."

"I'm done, anyway." She picked up her buckets and headed his way. When she got close Beck gave her an up and down glance.

"I know, I know. You were right. I'm filthy."

"That's what you get when you dress to impress." Now that she'd gotten away from that mangy horse, Beck relaxed.

Aubrey slowed a few feet shy of the fence. "Hi, Dani."

Dani climbed down in record time and took off running toward the barn. Beck wasn't worried because Cassidy was in her office.

"Seems like we both have some groveling to do." The sadness in her voice about broke his heart.

"Seems like. I'll return the buckets if you want to go clean up. Washer and dryer are back behind the kitchen."

Aubrey sniffed her sleeve. "I do smell like a horse, don't I?"

"Look a bit like one too, at the moment."

She chuckled as she walked off, and that sound kept Beck smiling for a long while after.

~~~

At loose ends after putting her clothes in the wash, Aubrey wandered around the kitchen. She had no idea who cooked what meals, but she remembered a huge plate of sandwiches in the kitchen before lunch hour the day before. Peeking inside, she didn't see any sandwiches.

Did Beck do all the cooking?

Maybe she could help. She searched out all the fixings and soon had a plate of sandwich halves piled to about as high as she remembered. She covered them in saran wrap and whipped up two pitchers from the thawed lemonade concentrate in the fridge. There were two more pitchers in the cupboard, so she rooted around for some tea and soon had sun-tea setting outside to steep.

Feeling good, she went upstairs for a well-deserved soak.

A soft knock at the door woke her. How long had she been in there? The hot water had turned tepid.

The knock sounded again.

"Yes?"

"Are you all right? You've been in there a while," Beck said.

"Yes, yes, I'm fine." Except for the things your deep voice does to my psyche. "I guess I fell asleep."

Beck cleared his throat. Was he thinking of her, in there? Aubrey's whole body tingled at the thought.

"Well," he continued. "Everyone's eaten and gone back to work. Thank you for the sandwiches and lemonade. You didn't have to do that."

"I wanted to help out."

"It was nice. Saved Cassidy some work, too."

Cassidy makes lunch? Aubrey felt even better about
~~~

what she'd done.

"I saved you some."

"Great." She sat up, the water sloshing.

Again, Beck cleared his throat. It was a while before he spoke, but his gruff voice had returned. "Make sure you're in the arena by 2 p.m. sharp. Don't have Sadie saddled. We'll give your sore legs a rest and work on saddling today." His footfalls down the hall put the exclamation point on his statement.

Nothing was ever easy with this man, Aubrey decided. Since the water had cooled, she got out and slipped into clean jeans, feeling much better, though next time she'd wait until after her lesson to wash clothes. Beck had been right. She'd dressed to impress earlier and now her whitest, newest tank would never get cleaner than dingy ivory. Ranch life.

This time, she put on her oldest tank top, even though it was too clingy and the yellow had faded. She'd change after her lesson. As she walked into the arena, she saw three saddles astride the fence and a huge, unfamiliar horse standing next to them. Dani hung over the top rail in what seemed to be her favorite position. Aubrey waved at her. Dani didn't wave back, but she didn't scowl, either. Aubrey counted that as progress. She glanced again at the saddles. They were bigger than she remembered. Sitting on the fence instead of on horses, they looked even larger.

"My arms will pay for this, I'm sure," she muttered. "This ranch thing is going to kill me before I'm done."

Beck walked Dani's pony and Sadie into the arena, his tight t-shirt moving with each muscle.

"Give me strength," Aubrey muttered.

And that was exactly what she needed. Once Beck tied the horses off inside the arena, he leaned against the fence rails, his eyes intense as they inspected her jeans. He gulped, righting his gaze. "Know how to saddle a horse?"

That lazy smile of his distracted her. "It's, umm, been a while."

"Let's start with Sam, then."

Dani's pony was small in stature. Sadly, that didn't apply to the saddles. Following Beck's directions, Aubrey placed the saddle blanket on Sam's back.

"Make sure it's high enough that it covers the withers. That way, the saddle won't rub against him."

Aubrey resettled the blanket and looked at Beck. When he nodded, she tried to figure out which saddle to use for Sam.

"They won't walk over there by themselves," Beck said, not moving from his post at the fence, right next to a grinning Dani.

Fine. If that's the way he wants to work it. Aubrey reached for the smallest saddle, though not by much, and locked the girth and stirrup over the horn so they would be out of the way. Then she hefted the saddle. Okay, maybe those workouts at the gym were doing some good. This didn't feel too bad.

She walked around to Sam's left side. "Good boy," she murmured as she lifted the saddle and settled it on the pony's back. He barely moved.

"Make sure the horn is over the withers."

Hence the blanket shift so it wouldn't rub. Aubrey bit back a retort. Once she had the saddle settled in the right place, she freed the stirrup and girth from the horn.

Beck joined her as she reached beneath Sam to grab the girth strap. She fed the cinch strap through the saddle ring. Damn. That was about all she remembered.

"I'm not sure how to run the strap so it's tight."

"Okay," Beck said, stepping in. "Here's how. Feed the strap around again and secure it like this." He made quick work of finishing the cinch. "Be sure to tighten the cinch again, snugging it up. Don't want that saddle falling off." He walked around the horse, tugging here and there. "You did well. The cinch buckle is above the shoulder so it won't rub Sam as he moves. The placement is good. All in all, a good first saddling."

More pleased than she expected to be, Aubrey patted Sam's neck and grinned. "Thanks."

Beck motioned to the two other horses. "One down, two to go."

"You're kidding, right?"

He grinned. "Best way to learn is by repetition."

At five foot five inches, Aubrey was about average height for a woman. But getting a saddle over Sadie, not to mention over the behemoth Beck rode, would be almost impossible. However, unwilling to give Beck the satisfaction of her failure, Aubrey walked to the saddles. "Which one's for which horse?"

Beck pointed, and Aubrey picked up Sadie's pad and walked over to the horse, who nickered as she settled it in place. "Good girl. You've been through this before, eh? Me, I'm a greenhorn. But I'm learning and I'll try not to hurt you."

Back at the fence, she prepped Sadie's saddle. Testing its weight, she found she could carry it pretty well, but she knew she'd never be able to get the saddle up on Sadie's back. Not without practice. Sadie was a tall horse.

Before she could reason out a solution, Beck lifted the saddle from her arms and placed it on the horse, shifting it until it was in place.

"Thanks."

He chuckled. "I want you to learn. Doesn't mean I'm an ogre."

Smart won out as Aubrey compressed her lips to keep

from refuting that statement. Besides, when he smiled like that, it was pretty hard not to smile back.

"Show me your moves, beautiful," Beck said, his voice a low thrum that eased its way past her defenses.

Beautiful? He thought she was beautiful? Heat suffused Aubrey's cheeks as she leaned against the horse to keep herself from leaning toward Beck. "My ... moves?"

He surprised her by closing the distance between them. He placed a hand on Sadie's haunches. If he put the other one on the horse's neck, Aubrey would be trapped.

Bending down, his lips were so close to her ear that his warm, inviting breath teased the hair on her cheek. "Yeah, you know. Your saddling moves."

Aubrey shivered, unable to stop herself. "Kind of hard to, with you all up in my business."

"It's a pretty nice place to be, now that I'm here."

Aubrey's brain died completely. Not a single word or retort came to her. All she envisioned was doing business ... with Beck.

When he backed up so she could see his face, all merriment had fled, replaced by dark eyes, flaring nostrils, and intensity. Something had changed, for both of them. She wanted to reach up and feel those rippling muscles, remove that shirt and run her hands over his warm, tanned skin.

She must have sighed because his eyes dipped to her lips. God, she wanted more than his eyes on her. It figured Hope would have a smoking hot brother.

Hope.

All the fire in Aubrey's veins died as her friend's image filled her mind. She couldn't do this. Couldn't betray the memories or forgive what he'd done.

Beck's expression grew confused, then devoid of any emotion as he backed away from her.

"Finish with Sadie, then I'll help you saddle War Horse." He strode back to the fence where Dani still watched them.

Just like that, her world righted itself. It was better this way, though Aubrey missed the warmth of his breath and ached for his touch. Too bad for her. He was forbidden fruit.

It didn't take long for Aubrey to saddle the two horses. After that, she took to the sidelines while Beck put Dani and Sam through their paces. Dani knew her stuff. She rode better than Aubrey, like she'd been on a horse since she'd learned to walk. That couldn't be true, though. Beck had only bought this place and brought Dani here a few months earlier.

Beck said something to Dani, who laughed, causing both Beck and Aubrey to freeze and listen to that golden sound. It ended as quickly as it started. Dani clapped both hands over her mouth and glanced skyward. Her balance off, she canted to the side. Even though Beck was right there to catch her, Aubrey was halfway across the arena by the time he'd pulled Dani into his arms.

"Never, never lose your focus, child. Never."

Aubrey squinted at the harshness of his tone. Dani didn't cry, though. She nodded her head solemnly until her uncle set her down.

"That's it for today, Dani. I'll take care of Sam. Go find Cassidy, all right?"

She nodded and raced to the fence, climbing it in record speed. She was gone before Aubrey joined Beck in the center of the arena.

"There's a lot going on in her head, eh?" she said.

He continued to look in the direction Dani had gone. "Agreed. It's hard to find all the pieces to her puzzle." He shook himself and quickly removed the frown that touched his face. "You've had an influence on her."

"She won't come near me."

"Still, she's aware of you, and curious. Interested, even." He glanced again in Dani's direction, then back at Aubrey. "Would you be interested in going for a ride tomorrow? It wouldn't be for too long. I recognize you must still be pretty saddle sore."

Oh, boy, was she.

"Here on the ranch?"

He nodded.

"With ... with you?"

"With me and Dani. I think it would be good for her."

"Can I ride Rudy?"

There came that familiar scowl. "No."

"When will I be able to ride him?"

Beck ran a hand through his hair. "I'm not sure, but no open range until I see you up on him in the corral. Got that?"

Not the answer she'd hoped for, but he was right. She hadn't even saddled Rudy yet. "All right. I'd like to go riding tomorrow."

He gave a quick nod. "Good. Right after lunch, then. Instead of lessons."

Picking up Sam's reins, Beck led the horse to the gate and opened it. He untied Sadie and grabbed War Horse's reins, leading all three out. "See you tomorrow," he said over his shoulder, leaving Aubrey alone in the arena.

With no horses, the arena seemed larger. She took a deep breath, trying to settle the emotions stirred up in the past hour. Aubrey didn't want to stay away from Beck, yet she must. She wanted to get on Dani's good side, yet for every stride forward they made, it felt like she took three giant leaps back.

And now she was going riding with the two of them

tomorrow.

Mara, what were you thinking, sending me here? Mara. That's what she needed. A nice, long, explanation-filled conversation with her friend. Beck texted with his men, so there must be wifi or something she could access.

She turned to leave, intent on finding a way to call her supposed friend. A glint caught her eye and she bent down to find a heart pendant on the ground. Bigger than what a six-year-old would wear, but where else could it have come from? She turned it over. It looked familiar. Opening the catch, tears came to her eyes when she saw Hope's picture, and baby Dani's on the other side. This was the locket Hope never took off. Aubrey smiled through the tears, glad beyond belief that Dani owned it now. It must be precious to her.

Aubrey walked to the barn. She found Dani sitting cross-legged at a coffee table in Cassidy's office, working on lettering sheets. "Dani, honey, I found this in the arena." Aubrey crouched down and dangled the locket.

Dani's eyes widened and her hand flew to her throat. She took the necklace from Aubrey with a reverence unusual for a child so young.

"I remember your mother wearing that locket. I'm glad you have it, kiddo. I loved your mother, too. Very much."

Dani stared at her, perfectly still. Suddenly, all the fear disappeared and she launched herself into Aubrey's arms. They plopped to the ground and sat there, hugging and crying and grieving together. Aubrey caught movement out of the corner of her eye as Cassie slipped out, closing the office door behind her.

The flood of grief carried them for a long time. Aubrey didn't know what words she spoke, only that they soothed Dani, soothed herself. Finally, she could hug the child she loved so much. Aubrey sent a gratitude-filled prayer skyward, then settled in beside Dani at the coffee table, pointing, and watching her work her letters.

No words were spoken.

And even though Aubrey wanted desperately to hear Dani's shy, endearing voice again, right now, no words were needed.

The call to Mara was forgotten.

Aubrey had come home.

CHAPTER TWELVE

Beck spent the morning with the breeder whose endorsement he was pursuing. By the time Grayson Myers left, Beck had been well-tested. He'd answered more questions about ranching and breeding than he thought he could. It seemed like it went well. The man was open to not only selling Beck some stock, he suggested he might even recommend him to clients. Beck would find out soon enough. Plus, he still needed to register with the American Quarter Horse Association. Thankfully, he had enough funds to wait the process out.

Boy, did he need some downtime. While scheduling a ride this afternoon wasn't the smartest thing he'd ever done, Beck looked forward to letting the ranch be for a while to enjoy a ride with Dani. Time with Aubrey lured him as well. As much as her stubbornness pushed his buttons, the attraction between them had not gone away. In fact, his had only gotten stronger, but his head wasn't in the right place for a relationship, and Aubrey deserved nothing less. Not that she seemed any more ready than he did.

Maybe, though, for this afternoon, they could put their differences aside and just enjoy themselves.

He pulled his hat off and wiped his brow with a glance at the sun. Looks like, if he wanted this ride to happen, he'd better get a move on. He headed to the house for a good wash up.

Aubrey and Cassidy were in the kitchen. Beck stopped beside the door to watch.

"That movie had nothing to do with the truth. It didn't happen that way," Aubrey said.

"Who cares if it's the truth or not. It's really all about that hunky lead actor." Cassidy spread a hand across her chest. "Be still, my heart."

They laughed together, Cassidy's low and throaty, whereas Aubrey's lit the room with sunshine, lightening Beck's mood and bringing a smile to his own face. "What hunky actor?"

Both women yelped.

"Boss. We didn't see you there."

"Obviously." He joined them. "So, who's this hot actor?"

They dissolved into a fit of giggles. Beck never got his answer, though he didn't care one bit. Their joy made his day.

Aubrey wiped tears from her face. "We're about done here. We left you some lunch in the fridge. And we've packed a snack basket to take on the ride."

"Sounds good. Let me get a couple things done and I'll meet you in the barn in about twenty minutes?" He reached in the fridge, pulled out a sandwich and took a big bite.

Aubrey nodded. "See you then."

Eating while he climbed the stairs, Beck cleaned up

and changed shirts, unwilling to examine why he chose to spruce up before a dusty horse ride.

On his way to the barn, he reminded Cassidy to go to her father if she had any questions that afternoon and grabbed a walkie-talkie in case there were issues. When he saw Aubrey and Dani walking ahead of him, Beck stopped dead in his tracks. They were hand-in-hand, his niece skipping along beside Aubrey. Actually skipping.

How had that happened? His niece seemed happy, at least, from what he could see. Beck hurried to catch up, grabbing Dani's other hand, surprising them both.

"You two are getting along pretty well," he said.

"We had a bit of a breakthrough yesterday after lessons."

"You'll have to tell me about it sometime. No words yet?"

Aubrey shook her head.

They swung Dani along and the girl's grin was wide and filled with teeth. It melted Beck's heart, seeing the joy on his niece's face.

"What, no saddles waiting for me to practice with?" Aubrey said as they entered the barn where Sadie and War Horse stood ready and waiting.

Beck shook his head. "I asked Amos to saddle them for us. Figured today's more about relaxing than learning."

Aubrey smiled and the puddle around that melting heart of his got bigger.

"No horse for Dani?"

"Too hard for Sam to keep up. She'll ride with me."

They walked the horses outside. Beck helped Aubrey seat herself, his hands lingering on her leg as she smiled down at him. His own grin widened in response. Next, he settled Dani and swung himself up behind her.

"Ready?" he said to Aubrey, unwinding his reins from

the horn.

She shifted a bit in her saddle.

"Still sore?"

"Not much. And not enough to want to stay back. I'm looking forward to this."

They rode out behind the barn and past the arena. Rudy's corral was in the opposite direction. While Beck didn't think the horse would be prone to jealousy, he didn't want to put a wedge between him and Aubrey when things were going well. He'd opted to steer clear of the horse.

Aubrey craned her neck right and left while they rode, taking everything in. Her curiosity gave him a fresh view of his land. Sweeping views of low rolling hills gave way to trees, the gateway to the mountains off in the distance. Now that he'd come back home, he couldn't imagine living anywhere else.

"How big is your ranch, Beck?"

"A little over a hundred acres. Not very big by Montana standards."

"Seems huge to me."

"Most of it is fenced, but there are gaps to allow the cattle to range free, thanks to an agreement among the ranchers in the area. So far, that hasn't caused any problems. I hope it doesn't, because I'd like to bring in some cattle later this year."

"Horse-breeding, cattle, a bed-and-breakfast. You have a lot of plans for this place."

"Yes, and some of them are happening sooner than expected."

"Meaning my arrival?" She batted her eyes.

Beck laughed. "Cassidy said she told you we brought furniture up from the bunkhouse. New stuff arrives in a couple weeks."

"Then you'll be open for business?"

"I don't know. The B&B thing was her idea." He still didn't know what to think about it.

"It's a good one, a shot at bringing in some money if your other ventures need time to take off."

He shrugged. "I'm worried I've taken too much on at once, that I've overstretched. Maybe I should focus on one thing at a time."

"I can understand that, but it's only a problem if you're finding yourself without the time to complete anything."

"We're managing so far, thank goodness."

Dani pointed, and they stopped to look at a herd of elk resting in the shade of some trees.

"Smart elk," Aubrey said, pulling off her baseball cap to wipe her brow.

They rode along in companionable silence. Aubrey was a natural around people. She seemed content with either conversation or quiet. He could see why she'd be good at her job. Anyone could be comfortable being themselves around her, with no need for airs or graces. Exactly like Hope. His sister made others feel at ease. Or had. Beck scowled, unable to stop his dark thoughts. Guilt, remorse, everything hit him with renewed vigor, reminding him he didn't deserve to be happy.

"You all right?"

He started, causing Dani to turn and look at him. "I—" Should he do it? Ask the question he'd wanted to ask since he'd found out who Aubrey was? An unusual fear gripped him. Did he really want to know?

"Would you tell me what my sister – what Hope was like, during her illness?"

Aubrey wobbled so hard on Sadie that Beck reached over and steadied her until she found her balance. She reined Sadie in and stared at Beck, her face a mixture of surprise, grief, and anger. If the downturn of her lips was any indication, anger would win the day.

"I asked too soon."

"Too soon?" Aubrey glanced at Dani. She spoke low, through gritted teeth. "More like too late. You could have seen for yourself, what it was like for her. Yet you ask me to fill that gap?"

Beck stared down at War Horse's mane. He had no idea what to say. When Aubrey spoke again, her voice was a little softer.

"You haven't shared the reason you weren't there. Why should I tell you anything?" She glanced at Dani again, who shifted her gaze between the two adults.

"Good point." Beck gazed into the distance, still not sure how to explain it, or if he even should in front of Dani. "I get that this should be a two-way conversation and I haven't been very forthcoming. I'm not ready. To be honest, I'm not sure I ever will be."

~~~

Aubrey wanted to scream at Beck. To tell him that nothing could excuse his absence from Hope's life. He'd missed so much. He didn't deserve to learn anything about her. If Aubrey hadn't seen how good he was with Dani, she'd say he didn't deserve custody, either.

But she couldn't say anything now. Not with Dani there. "Did you bring me along with the hope you'd catch me with my guard down?" she asked, even though the look of surprise on his face pretty much answered her question.

"I did not."

Aubrey nudged Sadie into a walk, War Horse falling in beside her. Beck seemed to be waiting for her to make the next move. How could it hurt to tell him bits and pieces of Hope's life? Maybe ... She watched Dani, who stared straight ahead now. Maybe she could share her perspective with both of them about Hope's last few months. She
~~~

leaned over and tapped Dani on the shoulder. "You okay with this, kiddo?"

Dani nodded. Permission given.

"The most important thing in Hope's life was Dani." Aubrey smiled at the girl, whose tentative smile in return said this might not be easy for her. Aubrey needed to keep a close eye on her reactions and stop if anything upset her.

"She'd enrolled Dani in pre-school in advance of kindergarten. Oh, will Dani start kindergarten this fall?"

"First grade. She's already enrolled. She's bypassing kindergarten, though she'll still be older than most of the kids."

Aubrey nodded. "Hope's energy was never so strong as when Dani walked back in the door from school." She smiled again at Dani, a smile as bright as she could make it. "She waited for you the entire time you were gone. She loved hearing what you learned, who you played with. And your artwork! Remember how we plastered it all over your mother's room?"

Dani nodded so hard, Beck had to hold on to her.

"Those walls were filled with color. All signed by the artist – you. And all dated." Where had those gone? Aubrey hoped and prayed they hadn't been destroyed. She didn't have any idea who'd cleaned out the house.

"I have boxes of Hope's. I need to go through them, maybe find some of that artwork." Beck's voice was quiet, thoughtful. He cocked his head toward Dani. "Would you like to put some of them up on the wall? Maybe in your bedroom? And my office?"

Her even more boisterous nod made them both laugh.

"That devotion went both ways. Dani would hop onto her mother's bed as soon as she got home, full of things to tell her. They'd sit there until dinner, discussing their day. Later, Hope, for as long as she was able, put Dani to bed herself. When ... when she couldn't anymore, Dani snuggled with her before bedtime. Do you remember how often you fell asleep right there in your mother's arms?"

The solemn look on Dani's face matched her slow nod.

"She loved you more than anything, kiddo. Do you remember what she used to say?"

Dani looked up at the sky but only nodded in response to Aubrey's question.

"She said she loved you more than a horse has hairs on its body."

Aubrey chanced a glance at Beck, surprised at the sheen in his eyes. Giving him his privacy—for now—she took in the view. At any rate, that was probably more than enough for Dani today. "This place goes on forever. Are we still on your property?"

Beck cleared his throat. "Yes."

"I guess I understand Montana's motto better now. This is definitely big sky country."

Beck turned War Horse. "There's a watering hole up ahead. Let's stop there and give the horses a drink and a break."

He reined in beside a tree near the pond, dismounted, and helped Dani down. Aubrey dismounted before he could assist her, since getting off a horse was easier than getting on. She reached for Dani's canteen and handed it to her, pleased when she took a long drink. She handed Beck his canteen before taking several sips from her own. Untying the kerchief around her neck, she wet it and put it back on, enjoying its coolness.

Before Beck took the horses to the water, Aubrey reached into her pack and pulled out the snacks she and Cassidy had prepared. Homemade chocolate chip cookies wrapped in cooler blocks to keep the chocolate from melting. Beck handed her a blanket. She spread it out and Dani plopped down in the center. Aubrey sat beside her. Beck joined them, taking the other side.

"Don't the horses need to be tied?"

He shook his head. "No. I just dropped their reins as a ground tie. They won't go anywhere. Besides, they know where their food comes from. Not like the wild mustangs."

Aubrey looked around. "Are there any here?"

"No. The few that remain have gone to the high country. It's cooler this time of year. But sometimes, in the winter, we'll see them wander through." He gazed out over the land. "I met a guy once. Sort of a horse whisperer. He spoke mustang, I swear."

"You mean, like neighing and such?"

"With horses, it's more about movements, which way are the ears turned, whether the legs are relaxed or stiff. You've seen some of this with Rudy."

"I definitely can tell when he's not in a good mood."

"That is the language of the horse. Did you know that head down is a submissive tell?"

"It makes sense."

"Well, I've tried that with him, to no avail. That horse just plain hates me."

"For now. For some reason we can't yet fathom," Aubrey said, though if a man had abused Rudy, it explained his dislike of Beck and any other male.

Dani tugged on Aubrey's arm and held out her hand, making both Beck and Aubrey chuckle.

"All right, all right. Cookie time." She handed cookies to each of them and bit into her own only slightly melted cookie. "Wow. These are superb."

Beck looked like he'd died and gone to heaven as he took a second bite. "They are the best I've ever tasted, God's honest truth. I can't get Cassidy to show me how she makes them, either. Says there's a secret ingredient, and she's keeping that to herself."

"As long as she keeps you in cookies, that's a fair bargain."

He grinned. "Exactly why I stopped asking her." His eyes dipped to her mouth. "You've got chocolate on your chin."

Aubrey swiped at it with the back of her hand, making Beck laugh. "All that did was smear it. Let me." He took a napkin and wet it from his canteen, then reached over and dabbed her chin.

His tender care almost undid Aubrey as amusement gave way to something much more serious. She stared at Beck and he returned it, desire floating in the dark depths of his eyes, waiting to be acted on. Her eyes probably sent the same message. She wanted him. He wanted her.

She leaned in. So did he. But with Dani in the middle, reality pulled them back before they acted on their needs. Because that's all it was. That's all it had to be. Aubrey wasn't ready to forgive Beck. And to sleep with him? Well, that wasn't fair to any of them, most of all Dani.

"Time to get back," Beck said with a full load of gravel in his voice. He jumped up and went for the horses.

Aubrey stuffed the cookie container back in the satchel, then stood. Dani got up too. "Help me fold the blanket?"

Together, they folded the blanket up small enough for Beck to cinch it at the back of his saddle. Without a word, he helped Aubrey mount, then lifted Dani up. Soon they were on their way back to the ranch house, the idyll of their afternoon disrupted by a history neither of them could get past.

~~~

That night, Aubrey found sleep elusive, with turmoil as
~~~

her bedmate. Everything about Beck drew her to him, yet he'd done something unforgivable. How could he never visit Hope until it was too late? The Beck she'd spent time with seemed so rooted in family. He doted on Dani. She'd seen him with Cassidy, with Amos, with the other ranch hands, easy and relaxed and concerned about their welfare. How did his desertion of his sister fit in?

Beck was as much a mystery now as he'd been four days ago, and he'd said he wasn't ready to talk about it. Aubrey wondered if he'd ever be ready. She should stay far, far away from him.

She gave up trying to sleep and went to the window. Pulling the curtain back, she gazed out at the dark night. So different from Seattle. Always a city girl, she'd never even considered country life. Too quiet, not enough action. Yet ... She leaned against the window frame. The peace of this place had an effect on her. She'd grown calmer. Maybe even a little less sad.

Rudy was down there, in his corral. Was he still miserable? Aubrey hoped that she'd been able to influence him and help him begin to trust people again. Otherwise, what would happen to him? He had such a good soul. He just needed to get past the pain of whatever had happened to him. Time. He needed time.

They all needed time, she supposed. Time and sleep, something she wouldn't be getting tonight, it appeared. She pulled on clothes and boots and tip-toed downstairs and out the door. She wanted to be near a kindred spirit. Once inside the corral, she searched the darkness until she found Rudy on the other side, down on the ground.

She moved slowly, unable to gauge his attitude, not wanting to spook him. "Hey, boy, it's just me. Mind if I visit for a while?" He didn't huff or shift, so Aubrey took that as a good sign. As she got close and her eyes adjusted to the darkness, she saw a lump against Rudy's side. Dani. Beck would be furious if he saw her there. Yet, Aubrey got it. There was something about this horse that drew them both.

"Dani, okay if I come sit beside you?"

She didn't expect a response, but she waited for a moment. When neither horse nor child bolted, Aubrey reached for Rudy's nose to pet him. "You're a good boy, aren't you, taking care of our girl, here. She's safe with you." She soothed Rudy, then moved between his curled in legs and settled next to Dani, leaning against the horse.

"All right if I hang here for a while?"

In answer, Dani curled into Aubrey, whose heart broke wide open, all the divots and corners previously filled with grief now flowing with love for her friend's child. So much had been lost, but so much gained in finding Dani. Aubrey cuddled with her, despite the day's leftover heat.

Dani lay her head on Aubrey's lap and stared up. Aubrey gazed at the stars herself, sending heart-filled prayers to Hope. "I miss her so much," she whispered.

Dani snaked her hand into Aubrey's as Rudy turned his head to them. The three of them lay there, looking at a star-dotted night sky, each paying homage to their emotions, giving them their head just for this moment, then letting them fly away to join the stars in the sky.

"We should get you to bed, Dani."

She didn't answer. When Aubrey looked down, she saw the girl was sound asleep, so she scooted out from underneath her and gave Rudy a quick hug. "Thanks for taking care of her, Rudy." She picked Dani up and managed to get through the gate and lock it behind her. Making it up the porch steps with a six-year-old wasn't easy, especially in the low light. Aubrey shifted so Dani's head lay over her shoulder. She made it inside the house and got the door shut, then trudged up the stairs, only to realize she wasn't sure which room was Dani's. She didn't want to open Beck's door by accident. "Dani, wake up," she whispered. "Which room is yours?"

Dani lifted her head and pointed to the one next to the bathroom. Aubrey eased the door open and, seeing a canopy bed with frilly lace lit by a bedside lamp, heaved a huge sigh of relief. She sat the girl on the bed and pulled off her boots. She'd worn her nightgown outside and now it was all dirty. "Sit up for a minute, kiddo. Let me get you a fresh nightgown."

With a close eye on the groggy girl, Aubrey rooted through drawers until she found a clean gown covered in tiny horses. She got the girl changed and into bed. Even though Dani was already asleep, Aubrey brushed the hair back from her forehead and leaned in to kiss it. "Sweet dreams, kiddo."

She picked up the dirty nightgown and boots and turned to leave only to have her heart hit her throat.

Beck stood in the doorway. In jeans with the top button undone, no shirt covering the ridges and lines of a well-muscled form, and the sweetest look of love for his niece on his face that Aubrey had ever seen. Already undone by her bonding with Dani and Rudy outside, her emotions broke open. Again. Dani's boots hit the floor with a thud, her dirty nightgown following close behind. Without thought, acting only on a need stronger than anything she'd ever felt, she walked into Beck's arms and they closed around her.

He barely got the door shut behind them before his lips crushed hers. Full of need and longing and everything good in the world. Aubrey met his kiss with abandon, fueling something she'd needed for too long.

He teased her with his tongue and she opened to him

gladly. They tasted and tested in perfect symmetry, neither able to stop. Somehow, they stumbled their way along the wall and into Beck's bedroom.

His hands slipped beneath her t-shirt, his calluses leaving burning trails up her back before moving down, following the curve of her buttocks and squeezing, pulling her into the proof of his need. She ran her hands along his back, reveling in the muscles that rolled and shivered beneath her ministrations. Smooth skin that shivered with light touches and relaxed with bold strokes.

Her t-shirt disappeared and they were skin-to-skin. God, he felt so good. So perfect. Aubrey breathed in his scent, kissed him like there would be no tomorrow. The back of the bed touched her legs. When had they moved? Aubrey broke the kiss to orient herself and froze. There, on Beck's bedside table, familiar eyes stared back at her, soulful and dark. The same eyes as Beck. Hope's eyes.

CHAPTER THIRTEEN

Blood roared through Beck, a sexual haze he'd never experienced before. Everything in his life fell away. All the angst and agony. Only Aubrey existed. Aubrey with the sun-kissed hair he wanted to wind around his fingers, whose warmth infused him with a sense of peace and heated him to the point of crazy. Aubrey, with breasts his hands were meant to hold.

She tensed. Something was wrong. His body thrummed with a feral need to have her. With difficulty, he reined it in, turned to see what she stared at. And all the warmth inside him died.

Hope.

Since Beck understood, he backed away from Aubrey, though it took every bit of strength he had to do so.

She sank to the bed, tears filling her eyes as she croaked out words. "I never noticed until now how you have the same eyes."

Picking up the picture, Beck ran his hand over the glass. "She was so beautiful."

Aubrey nodded.

"I keep her picture here to remind me how bad I screwed up."

"Why, Beck? Why didn't you visit?"

He fought the moisture in his own eyes and took a deep breath. In. Out. The pain consumed him again. He set the picture back on his bedside table and knelt before Aubrey, cupping her cheek with his hand. "I never want to hurt you. Ever. This is a discussion you and I need to have. Only ... I can't. Not yet."

Her eyes clouded over. He was losing her.

"Please." Beck never begged, but he did now. "Give me some time. God, Aubrey— " He stood and raked both hands through his hair.

Her eyes dipped to the erection that even this amount of pain couldn't quickly quash.

"Honey, I care about you. And things are different with you here. But I'm not there yet and I'm asking you. Please, give me some time."

"It's been six months, Beck."

"You arrived here four days ago in as much pain as I am now."

She winced. Beck wanted to smooth those lines away. Instead, he stood still, waiting like a condemned man about to receive his judgment. He hadn't realized it until that moment, but Aubrey had become important to him.

She stood, reached for her t-shirt, pulled it on. She stepped into Beck's personal space and stared up at him for a long time. He didn't look away. He'd been honest with her and needed her to see that truth.

When she set her hand over his heart, it jumped.

Aubrey smiled. A small smile, but enough to give him

hope.

"We're a pair, aren't we? I get it, Beck. I understand needing to deal with things in your own time. But this— " She waggled a finger between them. "This can't happen again until we have that talk. Hope was important to you. I see that in your devotion to Dani. Hope was important to me, too, and I need to understand what happened before I can move forward."

Beck let loose the breath he'd been holding. "Thank you." Covering her hand with his own, he leaned down and placed a single, quick kiss on her lips. "A reminder, to get us through." Then he walked her back to her room, giving her a second chaste kiss and standing there until she closed the door.

He glanced at his bedroom door. No going back there to sleep now. Beck headed downstairs to his office. After a fortifying shot of whiskey that didn't do what it should have, he tried to focus on financials for the ranch. The past six months had created huge deficits. He'd burned through too much of his base investment. If he didn't turn a profit within two years, all the money in his trust fund would be gone.

Unable to make sense of the blurring numbers, Beck slapped his desk and stood. He needed some action. Maybe mucking the stalls would help, though the horses might think he was crazy for the midnight disruption. He grabbed some carrots to appease them.

Outside, a soft whinny pulled his attention to the corral. Walking over, he put a foot up and leaned his arms on the top rail. Rudy stood about halfway down the corral, staring at him. At least he didn't race to the farthest point. Beck supposed that was progress.

"I could use a carrot, boy. Something to show that something, anything, I'm doing is right. Nothing seems to work anymore. None of us can figure out how to be happy." That wasn't quite right, though. Beck didn't deserve happiness. He'd committed the ultimate betrayal, and he'd spend the rest of his life trying to atone for it. "Want to throw me a bone, boy?" Beck reached into his pocket for a carrot. "Come on. All you have to do is step close enough to get it. I won't move. I promise."

Rudy didn't budge even an inch. He stood there staring at Beck with those sad, accusing eyes.

"You know, don't you? Somehow you know." Could that be why he and Rudy were at odds? Rudy knew his secret? Horses were very intuitive, and Rudy's own history attached him to Beck's mess. Rudy, Dani, Aubrey, and himself. All affected by a loss from which they might never recover.

Beck slapped the rail, causing Rudy to startle. This wasn't getting him anywhere. He tossed the carrot to the ground inside the corral and strode to the barn, intent on slaying his demons with hard work. After about an hour, he sensed someone watching him and turned around.

Dressed as if ready to start the day, Amos rested against the stall door, arms folded over his chest. From the cabin Beck had built to Amos's specifications, the man could see the barn and most of the immediate ranch area easily, so he'd have seen lights on.

"Got a problem you're trying to work out?"

Breathing hard, Beck leaned on the pitchfork. "Something like that."

Amos glanced around, probably noticing that Beck had gotten through three stalls already. He looked back at Beck and straightened. "All right, then. Be sure you get the corners good. Shit gets stuck there all the time." He walked off, presumably to go back to his bed.

Beck, who'd grown up mucking stalls, stared after the

man in amazement. He searched the stall he'd just finished. Damned if he hadn't left the corners undone. Shaking his head, he chuckled and cleaned them out, going back to the two other stalls he'd already done and taking care with those, too.

It took Beck another hour to get through the barn. Once finished, the satisfaction of a job well done dulled him enough that he fell right into bed.

~~~

"Absolutely not." Beck flipped pancakes as he wondered what the woman could possibly be thinking.

"Come on, Beck. You've seen how he reacts to me. We get along. If anyone can ride Rudy, it's me."

"I agree. But a lot more has to happen before you get on the back of that horse."

"But—"

"No buts." He pointed the spatula at Aubrey, momentarily muted by how the light from the window framed her face. "And no going behind my back, either. I'm serious, Aubrey. That will get you kicked off this ranch." He softened his voice at the hurt that showed in her face. "I'm responsible for the safety and well-being of everyone here. That includes you."

"I can handle myself."

He went back to flipping pancakes. "I know you can. You've already proven yourself. I spent some time last night thinking through a plan."

He glanced at her and saw the deep blush on her face, as well as the circles beneath her eyes. He wasn't the only one who'd lost sleep.

"A plan?"

"Yes." He put the pancakes in the warming oven and poured more batter on the griddle.

Aubrey pulled orange and apple juice concentrate out
~~~

of the fridge. Beck reached over her and got pitchers down, hyper-aware of how his hip brushed hers as he did so.

"So what is it?" she asked, emptying the concentrate into the pitchers and adding water.

"No matter what you think your relationship with Rudy is, horses don't change their color overnight. It takes a lot of work to convince them you are trustworthy. And that's where we'll start today."

She frowned as she stirred the juice.

"That is, if you think you have the stamina."

Fire filled her eyes as she looked up at Beck. Beautiful fire. "Bring it on."

"All right. We'll start when Dani goes to work with Cassidy at nine. No tank tops today. You'll be in the sun a lot. There's sunscreen in the bathroom. If you need a long-sleeved shirt, Cassidy might have one you can borrow."

"I can find something."

"Good."

"Okay." She picked up the pitchers and headed for the dining room, leaving Beck wondering what she had up her sleeve. She'd been way too agreeable. If Beck had learned anything in the last few days, he'd learned that this was the time to be most wary of Aubrey Gannet.

He flipped the last of the pancakes into the warming oven and started on eggs as voices on the other side of the door reminded him breakfast was overdue.

~~~

Sun beat down on Aubrey as she concentrated. Rudy watched her with wary eyes, so she stood still and let him get used to the saddle. They'd spent three days getting to this point. Day one had been all about the halter. Day two it took her three hours to get him to accept a blanket on his back. Today was saddle day and it wasn't going well.

Early on, Beck had explained the signs to look for.
~~~

Ears back and straight legs meant tense. The opposite meant relaxed, and Rudy was definitely not relaxed. Aubrey walked around the side and let the saddle touch Rudy. He shied away. She put the saddle on the ground and backed up. After a few seconds, she picked the saddle up again, walked closer. Each time he shied away, she started over. This was how she'd gotten the blanket on his back, by letting his reaction determine her action.

Stretching to ease the ache between her shoulders from hefting the saddle over and over again, Aubrey wondered how long she could keep this up. She left the saddle on the ground and moved closer to run her hands along his neck. "You're doing good, boy. We're not going to press you. Whatever happened to you, I want you to know it won't ever happen again."

She leaned into the horse. Somehow, in the days she'd been there, she'd come to equate the smell of horse with a sense of home. Of peace. Aubrey suspected that, when it came time to leave Hope Ranch, it would not be an easy thing for her to do. But sooner or later, she'd have to return to her life, and her job.

"You've both had enough of a workout," Beck said. He'd managed to get Rudy used to him being inside the fence rather than outside, but that was as close as the horse would allow him. As soon as Beck took one step, the horse bolted.

Aubrey shook her head as Beck joined her. "Baby steps, eh?"

He nodded. "He's come a long way already. He sure looks a good sight better. Smells it, too. Thanks to you."

The compliment pleased Aubrey. She wanted Rudy to be happy and it was gratifying to know she'd helped. Each day, after their work together, she brushed him down. One day, she hoped to give him a bath with a hose.

Beck slung the saddle over his shoulder.

"I can get that."

"You're about done in from lifting it so many times. I'll put it away."

He was right. Her shoulders were going to be screaming tomorrow.

"I'm working with Dani next. You've proven yourself capable, so you don't need more lessons. Want to sit in and watch?"

"I'd love that. I'll brush Rudy down then join you."

Beck nodded and walked off. Aubrey picked up the brush and met Rudy under one of the shade trees. She started with his neck and worked her way along his flank. Though Aubrey still took care around his hips and those scars, this had become a peaceful ritual for both of them. Rudy's eyes were closed and he seemed to enjoy the attention.

After finishing and letting Rudy find the carrot in her back pocket, Aubrey gave him one last pat, dropped her bucket off at the barn and headed over to the arena. Cassidy stood at the fence. She looked like a natural ranch girl. Jeans, boots, tank, and requisite plaid shirt. And wild hair that probably did not easily tame.

"Hey, Cassidy."

"Hey."

They watched Beck and Dani in companionable silence. His patience and her silent enthusiasm were occasionally at odds with each other, but overall they worked well together. And Dani clearly loved her pony.

Aubrey felt so lucky to be witness to Dani's joy. She didn't understand why the child wouldn't speak and prayed that a little more time would solve the issue. Beck, though. He was a whole other problem entirely. Aubrey couldn't stop thinking about his kisses. They'd come so close to doing something that might have damaged her. Severely. And she'd wanted it, bad enough that it scared her. Even now, she craved Beck. Wanted to be close to him, to feel him against her.

He glanced her way and his easy smile made her heart stutter. Aubrey smiled back, unable to stop herself.

"So," Cassidy said, watching Aubrey closely. "How are you liking ranch life these days?"

Silently cursing the heat that crept into her face, Aubrey kept her gaze on Dani and Sam. "It's a different world, for sure."

Cassidy laughed. "It is. Or at least, that's what I hear. I've never spent much time away from ranch life."

"Really?"

"Really. Dad's got a good reputation for helping troubled ranches, so we've moved from ranch to ranch."

"Are you all right with that?"

She shrugged. "It's all I know. But Beck ... well, it's different here."

"Different how?"

"Beck didn't just hire my Dad. Said he wouldn't unless my Dad became a partner. Gave him a stake in the business as well as a steady income. Even built him that cabin he lives in."

Aubrey had seen the small cabin at the back of the main property, with shuttered windows and painted a relaxing sage, with a plethora of flowers in beds and baskets. "It's a really cute place. I love all the flowers."

"They're my pride and joy. We're lucky the cabin is set back in the trees enough that it gets good shade."

"It looks beautiful. You've created an oasis."

Cassidy's nod was exuberant. "I wanted Dad to have something of me there, for down the road. I'll be graduating next spring. I'm applying to art schools, to get a degree and maybe do something professionally."

"Oh, Cassie, that's wonderful. If what I see in the house is any indication, you've got an amazing talent."

"Speaking of amazing things, how are you getting along with Beck?" Cassidy asked, glancing at her sideways.

Aubrey gripped the fence, trying to formulate an answer behind her dry throat. "Fine," she croaked out, clearing her throat to try again. "Fine."

"Just fine?" Cassidy laughed. "I thought maybe you guys had a thing for each other."

Even though Aubrey shook her head, the denial wouldn't materialize. She needed to distract Cassidy to get her off this bent. "Beck's good with Dani and I love her to pieces. She's the one thing we have in common."

"Feelings for someone have nothing to do with what you have in common. Remember that." Cassidy jumped off the fence. "I'm headed back to work. See you at campfire tonight?"

Aubrey nodded and waved, still unable to voice anything to discourage this idea that she and Beck could be ... anything. Too much lay between them. Insurmountable odds, which no longer seemed to provide an effective barrier to keep her away from him.

Beck smiled at her again. That small gesture sent every "steer clear" thought straight out of her mind, but she needed to be strong. For Hope. For Dani. And she had no idea how she'd accomplish that.

The other night shouldn't have happened. It had been a good distraction, though, given that Beck had never asked Aubrey why she'd been in Dani's room. Every night since had followed the same pattern. Going out before bed to see Rudy. Dani joining them. Getting Dani quietly into bed without disturbing Beck.

For that, Aubrey was grateful. While Dani's visits to

Rudy at night were fraught with danger, nothing would stop the child, so Aubrey joined her, keeping her safe just as Rudy did. She felt guilty about not telling Beck, but he'd put a stop to it and, for some reason, it was important to the girl. Maybe it would help her get past her own grief.

For now, she'd keep it to herself but would encourage Dani to give up her late-night forays. And hope that Beck didn't figure things out before she could convince the six-year-old to stop.

~~~

That night, well after the ranch had gone to sleep for the night, Dani crept out to Rudy's corral. Aubrey waited there for her. Together, they walked to Rudy's side. As with each of the past few nights, Rudy laid down, offering a soft belly for the two of them to cuddle against and stare at the stars. Only this time, she put a time limit on it. After about twenty minutes, she nudged Dani.

"You need some sleep, young lady." Aubrey stood and held out her hand, grateful when Dani took it and stood. Together, they said goodnight to Rudy, who watched them with those expressive brown eyes.

Back in the house, Aubrey tucked Dani into bed, constantly looking over her shoulder, praying Beck wouldn't show. She made it back to her room and closed the door behind her, letting out a sigh of relief tinged with a regret she didn't want to think too much about. She climbed into bed, completely exhausted after her afternoon working with Rudy, praying she'd drop off quickly tonight without thoughts of being pressed up against Beck's hard body.

Too late.
~~~

CHAPTER FOURTEEN

Beck straightened from where he'd been leaning against the house as Aubrey and Dani disappeared inside. He'd watched them each night, fighting the urge to forbid them to go anywhere near that horse. Dani found ways to escape that stymied him. He wouldn't be stopping his stubborn niece anytime soon, and since Rudy wouldn't let Beck get anywhere near him, he'd been relieved when Aubrey joined Dani. The woman drove him to distraction, but she had a good head on her shoulders. For now, all he could do was trust that.

He waited until he was certain Dani was in bed and Aubrey had retired to her own room before he crept upstairs and fell into his bed. Late nights and early mornings were not conducive to a happy rancher. Add the memory of Aubrey in his bedroom, half-clothed and so beautiful, and sleep remained elusive.

~~~

The next day tried his patience. Between equipment breakdowns and delayed feed deliveries, Beck's mood was foul as he headed for the arena and Dani's lesson.

"Hold up, boss."

"Amos, I've told you to stop calling me boss. We're partners. You're not my employee."

Amos shrugged. "Old habits. Anyhow, Sam's gone lame."

"What? How?"

"Took a look. No burrs or anything in his hooves. Checked his legs, too. Right rear one's warm."

"He's either out to pasture or holding a six-year-old on his back. How could he have injured himself?"

"Don't know, but I've called the vet."

"Good." He saw Dani racing toward him from the barn. "Guess I'd better tell her no lesson today."

"Okay." Amos walked off with a wave of his hand. Beck liked the man of few words immensely. When he'd sought him out to offer him a job, Amos explained that he'd been moving around a lot, and that Cassidy was about done with high school. Amos wanted to give her a home before she left for art school, a place to come back to. Beck had offered him a stake in the ranch, and it had been the best decision he'd ever made. Amos had held Hope Ranch together while Beck re-learned what it took to run a place like this. When they made a profit, and they would, Amos could build that retirement nest egg. He'd be welcome to live out his retirement right here, too. His friend didn't know it yet, but Beck had deeded Amos the land his cabin sat on, plus the acreage out to the main road. He only needed the right moment to tell him.

Dani threw herself up into Beck's arms.

"Oof," he said in mock injury. "To what do I owe this
~~~

burst of energy?"

Dani pointed behind her, at the arena. She'd grown to love being around the horses as much as he did, but some of them she liked too much.

"I'm sorry, sweetie. Sam's not feeling too good today. We need to let him rest for a while."

Dani's smile disappeared. She cocked her head, then squirmed to get down. Beck watched her race toward the house, returning moments later with a carrot in her hand.

"Want to go give your pony a carrot?" She always gave Sam one carrot at the end of lessons. Only one. Otherwise, Sam would be overweight, based on how often Dani tried to feed him. Beck chuckled as they turned toward Sam's stall. A second carrot peeked out of her jeans. He grabbed her hand. "All right, let's go feed your horse. After that, you can play in the office while I get some work done." He really needed to catch up on the business end of things. He'd spent way too much time working with Aubrey and Rudy and not enough on ranch-running.

Later, after Beck had finished cooking dinner, Aubrey and Cassidy said they'd do the dishes and kicked him out of the kitchen. So Beck used the extra time to help Amos set up that night's campfire, trying to reason out the changes in his life of late. Life on the ranch was no different, except for Aubrey. These last few days had been largely peaceful, mostly thanks to her. Domestic bliss. Without the benefits, that is.

And he wanted benefits. With her. He'd lain awake in bed aching for that but his timing was terrible. His head wasn't straight, his heart was mush, and his ranch and Dani needed his full attention.

The back door opened and Cassidy came out carrying a cooler of beer and lemonade, Dani beside her. He craned his neck to catch a glimpse of Aubrey as he took the cooler.

She came out last, carrying a ... guitar? Was there nothing the woman couldn't do? Every bit of her drew him in, and that scared him more than standing in front of a raging bull in a clown outfit.

"You play?" he asked as she joined them.

"A little. Nothing fancy. A few songs I used to play for my clients."

"I'd like to hear them."

"I'm trying to get up the nerve. In a living room with two or three people is one thing. Here— "

"You've made friends here. I'm sure everyone will want to hear you play."

She sat down on a log and Beck grabbed a couple beers and settled next to her. He popped the caps and gave her one as Dani sank into his lap. Soon, the entire ranch had joined them, more than ready to relax after a long day.

When the first chords whispered their way through the crowd, everyone grew quiet and listened to the song. Aubrey's voice joined the soothing strums of the guitar. A gentle song, full of happiness and peace. Her voice was true and as soothing as the music itself. Beck looked around. Some watched Aubrey, others stared into the fire. All had contented smiles on their faces. He knew his own looked the same.

For the first time in too long, Beck relaxed. He truly and deeply relaxed. Lulled by the music, sitting next to a woman he'd come to admire, and holding the niece he loved on his lap, his muscles unwound and his brain let go. For this moment, he could be here, nowhere else. Not mired in guilt, not worried about Dani or about the ranch, not fighting his attraction for Aubrey. He could just be.

Beck hugged Dani tight, and they swayed back and forth. Aubrey played two more songs before setting the guitar aside to a round of applause. He loved the blush that colored her cheeks.

Aubrey rubbed her fingers. "I haven't done that for a while. My skin needs toughening up."

Beck reached for her hand and pulled her fingers to his lips, kissing them, making Dani smile. "You are very talented."

"It's nothing. A little something I picked up. I take my guitar with me when I visit clients. It seems to soothe them." She frowned. "I didn't bring it with me here. I'm glad I found one in the house."

"It was my father's."

"Oh, I'm sorry. It must be something you treasure. I should have asked to use it."

He kept hold of her hand. "I'm pleased you found it and used it. That's what it's for. A couple of the hands play a little. They've borrowed it sometimes."

"Okay, then. I'm glad."

"So am I."

Aubrey hesitated for a moment, then leaned her head on Beck's shoulder. "This is nice."

"I agree." Beck felt more at home than he had in a long, long time.

Amos poked at the fire, sending a shower of sparks spiraling through the dark.

Looking down, Beck saw that Dani was fast asleep. "I'd better get her to bed."

Aubrey sat up with a sigh. "Need any help?"

Standing with Dani in his arms, he shook his head, then leaned closer to Aubrey. "Will you be here when I get back?"

She gulped, nodding, her smile timid.

"Good."

Somehow, Beck got Dani inside the house and into her bed without waking her. He pulled her shoes off and let her sleep in her clothes. They were clean. Enough. After drawing up the covers, he kissed her forehead. "I love you, sweetie," he whispered. And he did. It was hard to fathom, loving such a small person so much. He was awestruck by the power of his feelings.

He also sent a prayer skyward that she would, for once, sleep through the night. Beck wanted some time with Aubrey and keeping a six-year-old from sleeping with a cranky horse would not help with his plan.

Back outside, he grinned when he spied Aubrey still by the fire. Everyone else had disappeared.

"You waited."

"I said I would."

Beck nodded, sitting beside her and pulling her hand into his, cupping it within his warmth. Together, they stared into the fire, alone with their thoughts, but together in the desire to be right here and nowhere else.

"I want this," Beck said, almost as much to himself as to her.

"So do I." There was no quake to her voice, no indecision.

"It feels ... I'm not sure. Like it's not right. Not yet."

"Maybe this is what will make it right. Make us right." Aubrey turned to him, stroking his cheek with her free hand. After a brief pause at his lips, she looked into his eyes. "Funny how staring into a campfire can make things clearer. I was just thinking, about why I came here. Something brought us together, Beck."

"Mara."

She chuckled. "Well, yes. Mara. But something more. Fate? Or Hope. Maybe she sent us each other as a gift. To heal ourselves. To help her daughter."

"I like that idea."

Aubrey leaned in and kissed him, soft, like a whispered

promise. It broke him. Right down to his soul. Everything he'd been keeping in, holding back. All the guilt, the anguish, the pain, flowed out, leaving room for something he couldn't quite understand, except that it was ... beautiful. And yes, like Aubrey had said. Right.

He freed a hand and cupped her neck, pulling her in tighter. Deeper. Right where she needed to be. After what seemed like a peace-filled eternity, Beck broke the kiss and stood, holding out his hand.

Together, they walked to the house, up the stairs, and down the hall to his bedroom.

~~~

Hope's picture wasn't on the nightstand. It was the first thing Aubrey noticed while Beck closed the door.

"I moved her picture to my office." His arms encircled Aubrey's waist from the back. "Seemed more appropriate, and, well, I see her every day either way."

Hope. Was this fair?

Maybe not. But leaning against Beck fed something in Aubrey that had been missing for too long. Everything she wanted in a man lay wrapped in the complicated package that made up Beck Hawthorne, and she wanted to be there as he peeled back the layers of his own emotions. She wanted to love him through it all, starting tonight.

She turned in Beck's arms and gazed into his dark, intense eyes.

"You sure?" he asked.

Aubrey smiled. "I'm sure." She almost laughed at the breath he let out. He wanted this as much as she did, and that took her own desire to a heightened level. Emboldened by his lips, Aubrey reached for him as she had outside, pulled his head down, and kissed him. What had started out slow now quickened, became urgent as they moved to the bed.
~~~

She unbuttoned Beck's shirt and slid it off his shoulders. He whipped the t-shirt underneath off and tossed it behind him. This wasn't the first time she'd seen him shirtless. Still, he took her breath away. Aubrey ran her hands over his chest, exploring every angle and plane. A feather touch across his nipples caused a shiver he couldn't stifle.

He twitched when she ran her fingers along his side. "Ticklish, huh?"

Endearing. She moved behind him, watching his muscles move as she stroked them, keeping her touch light. This was more erotic than she'd ever imagined. It warmed her, heated her through, centering in a neck that wanted to be kissed, breasts that needed his touch, and an overwhelming desire for more. She sensed a lifetime with Beck would never be enough.

After circling Beck, she stood in front of him again, unsure after her exploration where to go next. He'd let her take the lead so far. Now, doubt snuck in about her limited experience in this arena and she stared at his chest, biting her lower lip.

Beck's groan pulled her gaze up to his intense dark eyes, bright with desire. He looked like a tightly wound coil of rope and Aubrey got the distinct impression that rope was about to uncoil in her direction.

"My turn," he said, his voice husky with need.

He slid the t-shirt up her torso with agonizing slowness, his calloused hands exciting the skin beneath. He raised it over her breasts, just touching the sides, sending need coursing through her.

"Oh."

"Should I stop?"

"No. No. Please don't." She arched toward him, wanting, needing more.

Her t-shirt disappeared over her head and Beck pulled her into him, showing her his need. Still, too much fabric stood between them. Her bra loosened as he unhooked it, and he drew back just enough to toss it onto the pile of clothing behind them. They came together again. Skin-to-skin, soul-to-soul.

Beck kissed her shoulder, moved to her neck. Every touch stoked her fire. Finally, when she thought she couldn't stand one more minute, he reached for the button on her jeans and pulled everything off at once. Soon, they were naked on his bed.

Running a hand over her body, Beck took his time, as she had, touching every part of her. He dipped his lips, following the route his hands had taken.

"Beck," Aubrey cried, overwhelmed with the sensations coursing through her. "I don't know how much more I can take."

He lifted from where he'd been paying close attention to her breasts, with his lips on one, his fingers on the other. "And we've only just begun." He teased her breast as he spoke and Aubrey arched into his hand, needing more. Needing him. She wrapped her hands around him, gaining a gasp and his undivided attention.

"Please, Beck. You want me as much as I want you."

"I do," he breathed into her nipple. "I also want to know you." He slid his hand lower, into the heated crevice between her legs. "All over." Soon, his mouth replaced his hand, and she flew off the edge of ecstasy, barely coming down before the next climax began to build.

"Beck," she begged.

He chuckled, reaching for a condom.

"Let me."

He handed it to her. Before she opened it, she wanted to savor him like he'd tasted her, a new experience. She moved lower, touching his tip with her tongue.

He jerked.

She grinned at the heady power, at the way she affected him with every simple touch.

Aubrey ran her tongue along his length, then pulled him into her mouth.

Beck groaned, holding her head, his entire body shaking with the effort to let her explore. She kept her touch feather-light, using her tongue here and there to amp up the sensations. Beck's hands moved to her back, running along her spine while she played. Until he couldn't stand it any longer.

He pulled her away from him, the light in his eyes mirroring her own fierce need. Aubrey opened the packet she still held in her hand, rolled the condom on, and came up to her knees to join Beck.

Beck's kiss was fierce, their tongues dancing as he lay her back down, then hovered over her. "You are so beautiful. Your skin, it's glowing."

"It's my desire. For you."

"Like mine for you. Only for you." He inched inside her, filling her deeper and deeper, tearing down every barrier as he went.

Tears rolled down Aubrey's cheeks and Beck pulled back. "Are you all right? Am I hurting you?"

She shook her head, finding it difficult to form words. "Overwhelmed. You. Wonderful." She croaked the words out, unsure how to express how he made her feel.

"I know the feeling. God, how I know." He settled inside her again, leaning down to kiss her with such sweetness, her heart burst open to let all the emotion, all her love for Beck flow into and out of her.

As the momentum built, she met every thrust with her hips, her arms, her heart. Another climax grew within her.

Beck paused.

"Don't stop," she begged.

"Open your eyes, sweetheart. I want to see you when you come for me."

She opened them, trying to show what she couldn't utter.

He moved slowly, every move, every look intense as he concentrated. Once, twice. Then he plunged into her, sending her into the chasm in a kaleidoscope of sensations, following her as he exploded with his own release.

They lay there, panting, clinging to each other as the euphoria abated. Beck moved to her side and Aubrey shivered. He pulled the covers up over her. "Give me a minute," he said, standing. "Please. Stay. I'll be right back."

Aubrey barely heard him. Now that the adrenaline had seeped from her body, movement wasn't an option. Nothing had ever felt like this, like she'd offered everything and been given even more in return. She'd never been so sated, body, mind, and heart.

She'd given her heart to Beck, though guilt tinged its edges. Aubrey glanced at the nightstand, searching for something no longer there. Someone no longer there. And the tears fell.

"Ah, honey," Beck said, climbing back into bed and pulling her into his arms.

"I'm … I'm s-s-sorry," she gulped, the grief hitting her out of the blue, washing over her like a river of choking mud. Aubrey clung to Beck, unable to stop now that she'd started. "I miss her so much. She was such a bright, shining star and now she's not here anymore."

"She's still that star, only we have to look up to see her now. And she's here with us. In our hearts. Always in our hearts."

"I shouldn't be happy." Aubrey gave voice to her

deep-seated fear. It felt wrong to experience such happiness when Hope had been so cruelly denied it.

"You shouldn't? You have every reason to be happy. Every right. Hope wouldn't want you to feel sad. She wouldn't want missing her to hold you back from living your own life. You knew Hope. You know what she'd want."

Aubrey nodded, clutching Beck's words like a lifeline to keep her from drowning. "You're right. She wouldn't like the sadness. She was all about making life fun and living it to the fullest."

Beck, silent for a long moment, held her tight. "I'd like to hear more about her when you feel like talking about it."

Aubrey turned her head so she could see Beck. "There's still one thing we haven't talked about. One big thing."

CHAPTER FIFTEEN

Beck forced his muscles to relax by will alone. If the distance Aubrey had just put between them was any indication, she'd noticed before he could stop his tension from showing.

"Please," he said. "Just ... give me a moment."

She settled back down, a comforting hand on his chest.

Could he do this? Explain what he'd done and risk losing Aubrey? Tonight had ripped his heart wide open. Everything swirled around inside, all the grief, remorse, love. He was naked, figuratively and literally.

How would she react? If he lost Aubrey now, Beck wasn't sure he'd survive. He'd come to care for her that much. Yet, if he didn't explain what happened, he'd lose her anyway. He didn't want to tell this story. Didn't want Aubrey to know. God, he didn't want to rehash his mistakes, though he pretty much did that already on a daily basis. Guilt followed him everywhere, always lurking at the edge of his sight, always threatening to tighten the noose around his heart.

Aubrey lay quiet beside him, waiting.

Beck sighed and kissed the top of her head, digging for the courage to say the words that might drive her away from him forever. He raked a hand through his hair, nervous, not sure where to start.

Aubrey pulled his hand to her lips, kissing it before she lay it on his chest, placing her hand over his.

"I grew up here."

"I know."

"You do?"

"Dani's social worker mentioned it."

"The people that bought it after our parents died ran it into the ground. It went into foreclosure about the time Dani came to live with me. Seemed like a sign."

"This must have been a good way to grow up."

"It was. We learned to take care of ourselves and to appreciate the satisfaction of hard work." Beck looked off into the darkness. "Those memories, those lessons, stayed with me. That's why I bought the place. I wanted Dani to have that life. Except she won't, because her mother won't be here to show her." He tried to keep his voice from shaking and failed miserably.

Aubrey squeezed his hand.

"I loved my parents. We had the best relationship. Same goes for Hope. She and I were close in age and the only kids on the ranch. We did everything together."

What came next would prove to Aubrey what an ass he truly was. Beck tried to pull away but she would have none of it. She held fast, telling him without words that she was here for him, that they'd walk this path together.

"What changed, Beck?"

"Everything. I went to college. Business degree. While

I was gone, there was an accident."

"Your parents?"

He nodded.

"It was winter. Their truck slid into a guard rail and down an embankment. No one found them for two days. By then, if their injuries hadn't claimed them, the frigid cold would have."

Aubrey hugged him tight. "I'm so sorry."

"I left for college thinking the only home I'd ever known would be here when I finished. When they died, all that was ripped away from me. I couldn't cry. All through the arrangements, the funeral and decision-making, nothing. I shut down. I didn't help Hope grieve, though she tried to cry on my shoulder many times." He gripped Aubrey's hand, pulling it tight against his chest. "I pushed her away, Aubrey. I chose not to deal with my grief. And ... I ran. As soon as I could."

He stared at the ceiling, not wanting to see her face, the hurt there. "I left her to deal with all of it."

"She never talked about that time. Said it was too sad and she wanted to focus on the here and now," Aubrey said. "But I didn't get the impression she was angry with anyone, or that she'd ever felt unduly burdened. You must have helped some."

"Only by phone, and even those conversations were brief. The burden lay on Hope's shoulders. I ... I poured myself into school, and after that, into my business. Grew it to a multimillion-dollar venture. I fought hard for that company so I'd have something to be proud of. Something to replace the grief, the guilt. But it was always there. I knew if I let go just once, the dam would burst and I'd never get it built again. I couldn't do it. I didn't want to feel that again."

"That kind of pain? I understand not wanting that in

your life, Beck. I struggle with it myself."

"At least you're working through it." He barked out a laugh. "I covered mine up, ignored it. I didn't return Hope's calls when she tried to reach me. I deleted her messages without listening to them. And then it was too late. I didn't know she'd passed away until the caseworker called me about Dani."

He wiped at unfamiliar tears. "All that time, I could have been with her, helped her. I didn't even know she was sick because I wanted to bury my pain. I was selfish, and I will pay for it for the rest of my life." God, would he pay. What he'd done was reprehensible. He'd left his only family to die alone.

When Aubrey shifted beside him, Beck let her go, steeling himself against the inevitable. She would leave him. She'd have to, after learning what he'd done. He deserved to be left. To be alone.

Aubrey sat up, pulling the sheet up to cover herself, everything about her looking closed off. She laid a hand on his chest. "That wasn't an easy story for you to tell, Beck, and I appreciate that you finally shared it with me."

She took a deep breath and Beck held his. Here it comes, he thought. The end of any chance I had at happiness.

"I wanted to bury those feelings myself. In all my time working oncology cases, I never fully understood what the people around me were going through until Hope. Once I did, it was awful. Basic day-to-day living became impossible to deal with. Every thought, every tear was for her. Except ... I didn't cry for Hope. I cried for me. For my loss. So even grief is selfish."

"It may be selfish, but it's natural," he said. "You've given yourself time to work through it."

"And you haven't."

Beck turned away. She pulled him back, her finger on his chin. He clutched her hand. He wanted to embed the memory of this moment in his brain. Her hand was so soft, so perfect. "I left her alone in the world because of my selfish need to be in control and bury my emotions. I know that's an insurmountable issue. You'll leave now. You have to, now that you know who I am." Despair ripped apart all the threads that longing had begun to sew together. Beck tried again to pull away, but Aubrey lay across him, forcing him to look at her.

Her gaze didn't waver as she searched his face. Beck stayed still, letting all the bottled up emotion show, giving her control. When she leaned forward, her cheek against his, he breathed in her sweet scent like a soothing balm.

Her voice, when she spoke, was no more than a whisper. "That's not the Beck Hawthorne I know. That Beck, that young kid, dealt with what life handed him the only way he knew how. I know you've got a lot of emotion bottled up inside, and you're just starting to let it out, but I'm glad you didn't know about Hope. Because, if you did, and you still didn't go to see her? That would have been difficult to swallow. I understand now. And I forgive you."

The sigh she breathed out was long and full of letting go as she wrapped her arms around his neck and held on tight.

Beck clung to her, needing her forgiveness like a horse needs water after a hard run on a hot day. He leaned into her comfort. "I'm not sure I'll ever forgive myself."

"I don't think you're asking for forgiveness from the right person." She kissed him, long and sweet, and then tipped her head, looking upward. "I think you need to have this conversation with someone else."

"She gave me that which was most precious to her. Dani. Did you know that?"

Aubrey's smile was tremulous, but happiness showed in her eyes. "I didn't. I doubt very much that Hope would have left Dani in your care if she hadn't forgiven you already."

Maybe she was right. Beck looked out his window, tried to glimpse the dark sky.

"Go," Aubrey said. "Find her in the stars. Talk to her." She pulled back, but Beck held on tight.

She smiled at him and cupped his face. "Don't worry. I'll be here, waiting for you. I love you, Beck Hawthorne. Now you need to love yourself."

With another kiss filled with forgiveness and love, Aubrey let the sheet fall and walked into his bathroom, giving him time to think. After she disappeared, he dressed slowly. The more he thought about it, the more he wanted to do this. It was time. He bounded down the stairs and was outside in seconds. He walked through the darkness, stopping only when he reached the corral fence, leaning on it, looking up.

"I'm so sorry, Hope." He let his tears fall. "I should have been there for you. Should have held your hand through everything. I never said goodbye. Never told you how much you meant to me." He poured his heart and soul into the conversation, the world around him fading as he gave word to the agony inside.

He didn't hear the horse approach, didn't realize Rudy was there until he felt the nudge. His arms slid around the horse's neck, clinging to him like a lifeline. Rudy leaned his head into Beck, the horse's acceptance the final key that unlocked Beck's tightly held emotions. Everything poured forth as he hugged Rudy. He talked to the horse, telling him about Hope's childhood, about the love of horses that had brought Rudy to her, and now to him. About how sorry he was that Rudy had been treated so badly.

"If Hope were here, she'd be kicking my ass for letting that man hurt you."

He took a deep, ragged, cleansing breath, though it was a long while before he separated from the horse. Even then, Beck was reluctant to leave, until a tug on his jeans got his attention. Dani stood next to him, smiling.

Beck picked her up. She touched his cheek then Rudy's nose, grinning at both of them.

"Yes, we're friends now. We found common ground. You, and your mom." Beck hugged Dani tight, letting tears of relief fall. Dani hugged him just as tight.

"I know you've been out here with Rudy at night."

Dani dug her face into his collar.

"It's all right. I've been watching to make certain you're safe. But it has to stop, sweetie. There are other animals that roam around. You know that. I don't want one of them to hurt you."

He set her up on the top rail of the fence. Dani put her arm under Rudy's neck and leaned against him.

"How about this? You and I come here every night before bedtime. We'll visit with Rudy, stare at the stars for a while. Then, when I put you in bed, you stay there. No outdoor visits on your own. Would that work?"

Dani scrunched up her face like she was thinking really hard, then pointed to the house.

It took Beck a minute to figure it out. When he did, he smiled. He liked this idea. "Okay, we can ask Aubrey, too. Will that work?"

Her nod almost shook her off the railing. Beck lifted her from the fence and together, they walked back to the house. He got her settled in bed and sat with her for a while, watching her as she fell asleep, so peaceful, so untroubled. He'd never known the kind of love he felt for Dani. It overwhelmed him, in a good way. His heart overflowed with emotion for this child. His sister's child, and now his.

Beck crossed the hall to his own room, exhausted by the evening's emotion and unsure how he would live his life with it all swirling around and inside him. He only knew he wanted to try.

He opened his door, relieved to see Aubrey still in his bed. Both the females in his life were sound asleep and something about that soothed Beck. Careful not to wake her, he slipped out of his clothes, turned off the light, and slid into bed, curling into her back.

She sighed, a deep sleepy, contented sound that pulled the last of Beck's tension from his body. Scant moments later, he slipped into his own dreams.

~~~

Dreams of curling up with a sexy man melted into reality when Aubrey woke with Beck's arms around her, his chest tight against her back. She opened her eyes, recognized his bedroom. The night flooded back, all the emotions, the way he'd treated her like something precious, how they'd talked. It had really happened. Ever since her arrival, she'd fought an attraction to Beck Hawthorne. No more. She understood now. Maybe not everything about him, but enough to know that he was a good man. Strong, caring, loving.

The kind of man she wanted to spend a lifetime with.

"Good morning," Beck said, tightening his grip for a moment.

She rolled over and stared into dark eyes she loved unequivocally. "Hi," she said with a hand over her mouth.

Beck chuckled and removed her hand, replacing it with his lips, eliminating any thoughts about morning breath. He nudged her hip closer to an awakening need, and Aubrey wanted to, so very much, but she glanced at the clock.
~~~

"Aren't you late to cook breakfast?"

"Crap. Yes." Beck sighed and kissed her deeply, giving Aubrey the unmistakable impression he was exiting the bed only with great reluctance. He slid out and pulled clothes on before leaning in to cup her breast. "You are so beautiful. I hate to leave you."

He kissed her again and Aubrey wanted nothing more than to pull him back under the covers. She let him go. A ranch depended on him. "I'll join you and help."

"Sleep in."

"No. I'm awake. And I can help."

"All right. But take your time. I'm used to this early morning routine. You aren't."

"I'm getting there, though. Go. I'll be down in a bit."

After he left, Aubrey stretched her arms overhead, enjoying Beck's bed and her memories. She pulled his pillow to her, still full of his scent, and hugged it tight. When she heard skillets settle on the stove below, she rose and slipped into her clothes. Opening the door just a crack, she saw that the hallway was empty, so she crept like a cat burglar to her bedroom door. Safely inside, she closed the door and froze, swearing another door echoed hers. Aubrey had no idea how Beck would feel if Dani found out they'd been together last night. She prayed she'd made it to her room without the child noticing.

After a quick shower, she dressed and headed to the kitchen, surprised that only Beck was up and about. He was in full swing, too. She joined him at the stove. Eggs, bacon, and pancakes were well on their way.

Beck stopped mid-pancake-flip and pulled her into his arms.

"Somebody will see us."

He grinned. "I don't care. Let them."

"Even Dani?"

"Especially Dani. Remind me later to tell you about my conversation with her last night." He kissed her, squeezing her in tight.

"You saw Dani?" Aubrey asked between kisses.

"We were together with Rudy."

"You? And Dani?"

"I'll explain later. If I don't watch these pans, breakfast will burn. Now go." He gave her a light swat on the ass. "Get yourself some coffee. Then check the juices and set out the plates and silverware."

"Yes, sir," she said, laughing. Pouring coffee, she added a liberal splash of peppermint white chocolate cream, because Cassie really had been right. Ranch coffee was strong. Aubrey took a sip, sighing with complete and utter happiness. She closed her eyes and listened. The only noise was Beck's work at the stove. No hustle and bustle, no cars, nothing. Funny, she no longer missed them. There was a peace in the silence. A peace she'd grown accustomed to in the short time she'd been there.

After making juice, Aubrey carried plates out to the dining room and set them on the buffet just as Cassie walked in, a wide grin on her face.

"Have a good night?" Cassie asked.

Uh oh. The girl knew something. "Pretty good," she said, trying for nonchalance. "I'm finally getting used to the quiet here. I slept well."

"I bet you did," Cassie said, laughing. She headed for the kitchen, presumably for coffee, but paused beside Aubrey. "I knew you two would be good for each other." She continued without waiting for an acknowledgment.

Good, because Aubrey's face flamed as she wondered how Cassie knew what had happened between her and Beck. Not one damn thing came to mind as she trailed behind the girl. When she entered the kitchen, Cassie stood by the coffee pot, cupping her mug, still grinning like she had a secret she loved knowing. Beck, turned toward the stove, didn't notice.

Oh. Lord. Give me strength. Aubrey rolled her eyes and nabbed silverware. She took the coffee pots to place on the warmers, then the juices. All the while, Cassie stood there and grinned at her.

Breakfast took forever. It seemed like everyone's eyes were on her, though all was normal except for Cassie. Dani kept looking between Cassie, Beck, and Aubrey like she knew something was up.

Apparently, there was no true privacy in ranch life.

When dishes were piled and ready to wash, Aubrey shooed Beck out of the kitchen. "I'll get these. You go do ranch stuff."

"Thanks." He leaned in for a kiss. "God, I enjoy doing that."

She drew circles on his chest with her finger. "Me, too."

"I'll help with dishes," Cassie said from the doorway.

Aubrey tried to jump back, but Beck would have none of it. He chuckled, and then kissed her again before releasing her. Tapping Cassie's hat, he told her to be nice and left Aubrey in the lion's den.

She filled a dishpan and began rinsing dishes. Cassie took them from her, loading the dishwasher in silence. Just when Aubrey thought she might get out of this with some dignity, Cassie spoke up.

"You don't need to be embarrassed. Everyone has been rooting for you and Beck since you arrived."

Aubrey turned to her, quite certain her eyes were like saucers. "Does the whole ranch know about last night?"

"No."

"Thank goodness."

"But there's a pool guessing when you two would hook up. So word'll get out."

"Oh. My. God." She hid her face in the kitchen towel she held.

"Welcome to ranch life, Aubrey." Cassie laughed. "Seriously, though, I've never seen Beck happy like he was this morning. You're good for him." She touched Aubrey's arm. "And I think he's good for you. You feel better, don't you?"

Aubrey sighed and set the towel down. "I do. A lot of that is because of Beck. But it's more. There's something about this place that ... settles a person. You know?"

"Oh, I get it. This place is more my home than any other ranch I've lived on. I love it here. It'll be hard to leave when I go to college."

"Hard, but important."

"Yes." She glanced out the window. "Anyhow, I've got more chores to do than these dishes. You mind finishing up?"

"Not at all."

"Great. Catch you later." She threw her towel over Aubrey's shoulder and left, though not without one last chuckle.

After cleaning out the last of the cast-iron skillets and drying them on the stove, Aubrey went to Beck's office for a long-overdue call to Mara.

"Where the heck have you been?" her friend asked, answering the phone almost before Aubrey knew the call had connected.

"At the ranch you sent me to. Where else?"

"It's been ten days. No, eleven. And you're just calling me now?"

"I needed to get over being ticked off at you before I called."

"Oh. Well, there is that."

"You sent me here."

"I did."

"With full knowledge that your cousin, Hope's brother, owned the place."

"I definitely knew that."

"And you didn't tell either of us who the other was."

"I did not."

"Why, Mara? Why would you do that to me? To Beck?"

"Let me ask you something first. Are you happy?"

"Don't change the subject. You manipulated me. And Beck."

"I can't answer you until you tell me if you're doing any better."

Aubrey paused. She didn't want to give Mara any leverage, but she didn't want to lie. "I wasn't, not at first."

"But you're happy now?"

Supremely, completely, giddily happy. "Things are getting better."

"That's why I sent you there." Her voice went quiet, like a whisper. "You needed to find your peace again. You were too stuck on Hope's death."

"We were all grieving."

"Not like you. You took her death really hard, Aubs. I was worried."

Aubrey couldn't argue. It still hurt to think she would never see Hope again, but now other emotions eased that pain. Love, and a renewed vision of future happiness.

"All right. I get it. I'm not happy about it, but you were trying to help, however underhanded it was."

"How's Beck doing? I was hoping you might help him, too."

Beck is amazing. Wonderful. He laughed this morning

harder than he had in a long time, according to Cassidy. "He seems to be pulling out of the funk he was in."

"I knew you would be good for each other. And for Dani."

"Yes, and that's what I'm really pissed about. You knew where Dani was and didn't tell me? Why, Mara?"

"Because I suspected you wanted to help Dani and right after Hope's death, when you were trying to find her, you were in no place emotionally to do that. Plus, I knew she was in good hands."

"So you took that choice away from me."

"I'll own that. You can hate me forever, but only if you can tell me this isn't working for you. That you're not on the path to healing, as well as Beck and hopefully, Dani."

Well, she couldn't say that. Honestly, everything had changed for Aubrey since her arrival. She'd found peace. Hopefully, even love. And Dani. Mara's heart had been in the right place. "I can't say this hasn't helped, but I don't like being manipulated."

"I understand, and I promise I won't ever do it again. Come on, though. You have to admit, my cousin is a good man. And a hunk to boot."

Oh, yes. Definitely a hunk. Absolutely perfect in every way, except for that "my way or the highway" thing. "He's ... nice to look at."

"Oh. My. God. You slept with him."

Aubrey put her hand to her flaming face, trying to cool it. She couldn't for the life of her come up with a single response that would put Mara off this train of thought.

"You did! See? You were meant to be together."

"We're not together." Yet. "But ... you're right, Mara. He's a good man. I, uh, I like him. A lot."

"There's no one better, Aubrey. I'd vouch for him any day of the week, even when he's being a stubborn fool."

"He told me about that time, about his parents' death and how he reacted to it."

"Wow. He's never told me the full story. You two seem to have found something special with each other."

"I'm afraid, though."

"Of what?"

"Of happiness. It still seems ... wrong."

"Give it time, Aubrey. That's all you need. Oh, speaking of time, it's back to work for me, but I wanted to tell you I'm coming to the ranch in a couple weeks. I want to see all of you, so I hope you'll still be there."

"I hope so, too. Don't work too hard."

Aubrey hung up the landline and walked to the window of Beck's office. She smiled to see Beck feeding Rudy a carrot, happy they seemed to have mended their differences. As had she and Beck. This thing between them scared her, especially since she'd fallen for him so fast. She'd learned that this kind of happiness could be fleeting. She'd already lost someone she cared about deeply. Would she survive if she lost Beck? And Dani?

It was hard to even contemplate, they'd become such a focal part of her life.

A truck roared down the driveway. Supplies? Or someone from the breeder? She didn't think Beck had heard back from him yet. Did they have more questions?

Beck turned and watched the truck skid to a stop. A man, big even by Beck's standards, got out and strode toward Beck with some papers in his hands. He handed them over without saying a word, from what Aubrey could tell.

The deep scowl on Beck's face as he glanced through the paperwork told her that whoever this man was, he wasn't bringing good news.

CHAPTER SIXTEEN

This now? After everything that had happened? Beck checked the back page, running his hand over the raised state seal. It looked legit.

"You're George Arenow?" he asked.

The man gave a curt nod. "I'm the owner and I'm taking him back."

Beck slapped the papers against his hand. "You abused that horse."

"I tamed him."

"He was already tame. You abused him so badly the authorities had to rescue him."

"They wrongfully seized him. That horse is part of my approved breeding program and I have a legal right to him."

Arenow leaned forward, unblinking and intense.

Beck stood his ground.

"I'm giving you a day's notice," the man said. "I'll be

back tomorrow with a trailer. Have him ready to go." He didn't wait for a response. He got back in his truck and tore out in a cloud of dust.

"Over my dead body," Beck spat out as the man drove off. He crumbled the papers in his hand then glanced over at Rudy, who stood at the far end of the corral, as far away as he could from Beck and Arenow. The horse had reverted to the shaking, wild-eyed look he'd had upon his arrival at the ranch.

"Not going to happen." He headed for his office to make some calls.

Inside, Aubrey waited. The worried look on her face showed she'd at least seen Arenow arrive. "What's happened?"

"He's the man who abused Rudy. He's got papers that say the horse is his. Says he's coming tomorrow with a trailer to take him."

"No!" Aubrey covered her mouth with her hand. Tears filled her eyes. "We can't let Rudy go back to that butcher."

Beck pulled her into his arms. "We'll fight this with everything we've got. He's not taking our horse."

"How can you be so sure?"

"Because I won't let it happen." He kissed her, soothing his own worry with her touch. "Listen, I need to make some calls. Find out if this is legit and how to fight it. Dani's normally with me when I'm at my desk. Can you distract her for a couple hours? She's been asking to see Hank's puppies."

Aubrey tried to chuckle. Since she couldn't manage it past the worry lodged in her throat, she shook her head instead. "How you never knew that dog was female is beyond me."

"She was feral. Wouldn't get close to any of us for a long while, and she has all that mangy long hair. One of the ranch hands named her Hank. It stuck."

"I'll find Dani and keep her occupied." Aubrey stood on tip-toes and kissed Beck again. "Make your calls and save Rudy."

"That's my plan."

After she left, Beck read the paperwork from front to back and then called to verify its legitimacy. Next, he spoke with the rescue group who'd brought Rudy to him. He called everyone he could think of. Two hours later, he was no closer to a solution.

When a gentle knock sounded on his door, Beck walked over and opened the door he rarely closed. Aubrey and Dani stood there, one filled with smiles, the other with her brow furrowed in worry. And rightfully so.

He gave a quick shake of his head, then picked Dani up. His smile wasn't faked. Having her there soothed his anger. Beck hugged her tight. "How are the puppies?" he asked, hoping, as always, that she'd answer with words.

Instead, she spread her arms out.

Beck laughed. "Getting big?"

Dani's emphatic nod answered that question.

"Everyone's eaten. We made lunch. Dani helped. She washed her hands good and put cheese on all the sandwiches." A small smile lightened the worry in Aubrey's face as another nod from Dani validated the statement.

"That's great, sweetie. Everyone does their part on the ranch. I know you understand that. I'm proud of you for doing yours."

Dani hugged him tight, and then he set her down. "Hey, can you be a big girl and go find Cassidy for your afternoon lessons? I need to talk to Aubrey for a minute."

Dani looked between them, her smile wavering. Her nod was slower this time but she left without complaint, walking toward the kitchen where Cassidy had clean-up duty.

Once she was out of sight, Beck shook his head. "I haven't had any luck so far."

"How can this happen?" Aubrey said, hugging herself. "He abused Rudy. How can the law back that man's claim?"

"Apparently, when the rescue organization took the horses from Arenow's stables, they should have filed legal paperwork before the horses were placed in foster homes. They did, for every horse except Rudy. He fell through the cracks."

"He's being sent back to that ogre because of a paperwork snafu?"

Beck scrubbed his face. "That's what the legal system says."

Aubrey paced back and forth. "I don't get it. Can't the rescue organization testify that he's abusive?"

"That's in process, but until it's completed ... well, innocent until proven guilty."

"Why Rudy? Why does he want this horse?"

Beck stared out the window. "When I saw the name Arenow on the paperwork it seemed familiar, but it took me a while to remember why. He and my parents wrangled back when I was a teenager. They hired him to provide the sire for a mare they wanted to breed. The day their mare was to be impregnated, they showed up at his ranch and were so aghast at how he treated the horses, they took their mare and filed a complaint. With nothing but their word, it didn't go far."

Aubrey clutched at Beck's t-shirt. "We can't let him take Rudy. We just can't."

"I'll be wracking my brain for ideas right up until he rolls in tomorrow morning."

"Oh, God. Me, too. Could we purchase him?"

"Because of our history, I doubt very much if the man will agree to that at any price."

"We could hide him. Refuse to hand him over."

Beck hugged her, kissing her forehead. "I wish it were that easy. It would be against the law and put the ranch in peril. I doubt George Arenow will agree to anything that won't yank me down a few notches in retaliation for my parents' complaint."

"I can't believe this is happening."

He breathed in her citrus-and-flower scent, trying to calm his nerves and clear his mind so he could find a solution. "Well, this isn't accomplishing anything. I'm going back to work. Maybe that will help me come up with ideas."

"I wish we could just go back to bed and start this day over. Maybe even back it up to last night."

That lightened Beck's mood. With one last, lingering kiss, he headed out to find Amos.

"George Arenow is no better than pig slop," Amos said.

"You know him?"

"By reputation and encounter."

"What do you mean?"

"I worked for the man. Twenty years ago, when I was breaking into this business. Saw how he treated his stock, so I didn't stick around long. Can't believe he's still in business."

"Did you know about my parents' complaint against him?"

Amos nodded. "Went to work for them right after that. I'd kept a journal. Gave it to them to help their complaint, not that it helped. The man's got some clout and, without more evidence, the complaint died without the prosecutor ever filing a petition with the courts. Never got a hearing and not a single animal was pulled from his stables."

A journal? That might be the exact thing Beck needed to put an end to this farce. It would remind the court of prior suspicion. Rudy's welts, along with the testimony of those who'd seized and brought Rudy to him, should be enough proof of the offense. Maybe they could finally put Arenow out of business. "Do you still have the journal?"

Amos shook his head. "Never got it back from your folks. Your sister might have kept it when she cleared the ranch out and moved to Seattle, but I've got no idea where it is now."

Beck hung his head at the reminder of all the work Hope had done. He couldn't take his inaction back and beg for a do-over. That was the past. All he could do now was keep everything important to her safe.

"Thanks, Amos. I need to go check on something."

He raced to the house and up the stairs to a room at the back, opening a door he hadn't been through since he'd moved the stuff in there. Never had the guts. Boxes and boxes filled the room. All of Hope's personal belongings.

He opened the first box and realized he'd failed again. Toys. Dani's toys. He'd been too mired in his own guilt to consider that anything of Dani's might be in there. Beck picked the box up and set it by the door. He'd go through it with Dani after this crisis was over. If they lost Rudy, this might help her feel better.

No. They would not lose that horse. Not now, after he'd finally forged a bond with the pinto. Beck dug in, opening box after box. So many mementos. Pictures of Dani that should be up all over the house. In the last stack, he found the box he'd hoped to find. Paperwork, like files pulled from a desk drawer. He dug through the pile, finding two journals at the bottom.

Beck recognized the crooked writing of his ranch manager. This was it! The best chance he had to save Rudy. He grabbed both journals and headed back to his office, silently promising to tackle the storage room as soon as he got things settled about Rudy. At his desk, he browsed the journal, then made three calls.

After he was done with the last call, Beck sat back in his chair, breathing, letting the stress go. Everything was in place. When George Arenow arrived tomorrow, he'd leave empty-handed, and Beck would have a signed a statement releasing all interest in Rudy.

If all went well.

Aubrey popped her head in. "Any luck?"

"I hope so. We won't know for sure until tomorrow, but I've finally got a few things in place that should help."

"Thank goodness." She leaned against the doorjamb.

Beck stood and walked to the window. "I feel like a month has passed in the last two hours. Nobody's hit me with any questions, so I'm assuming things are running smoothly today. That's rare."

"I bet. I'm heading to go get Dani from Cassie's office."

"Great. I'll walk with you."

As they stepped outside, a sedan drove up. Laura, Dani's social worker, got out.

Beck tensed without reason. Laura was a good woman, but it bothered Beck that she had the power to tell him how to raise his niece, and even *if* he should be raising her. Until Dani was officially his, he'd be under the microscope. He'd never tolerated things like that well.

"Hi," Aubrey said, shaking Laura's hand.

"Hello! I thought I'd stop by and see how things were going with Dani." She glanced between them. "You two seem to be getting along."

Beck held back a chuckle at the flush that blossomed on Aubrey's face. He made the smart choice and didn't respond to the statement.

"We were just about to get Dani. Want to walk with us?"

"Sure."

In the barn, Beck opened the office door but no one was inside. "Maybe they went to see Dani's pony. He's been lame."

At the end of the stable, Sam stood alone in his stall.

"She has to be with Cassie," Aubrey said. "Back at the house?"

All three headed there. Aubrey searched upstairs, Beck and Laura downstairs. They met again on the front porch.

"Where are they? Riding?" Aubrey asked.

"There's no way Cassidy would go for a ride."

"Right," Aubrey said. "She doesn't like horses."

"The only other place is Amos' house. Sometimes, Cassidy takes her there." Beck reached for his cell and called her.

"Yo, boss," she said, answering as she came around the corner of the house.

"Isn't Dani with you?"

"No. We finished her lessons, and she asked to walk back to the house by herself. Signaled that she was a big girl now. So I let her, though I watched her until she made it inside. I figured, with you being in your office, you'd see her."

"I was upstairs going through Hope's boxes."

"Oh." Cassidy frowned. "Then where is she?"

The recently unraveled knot in Beck's stomach yanked tight again. That knot exploded in a shower of acid as he heard Aubrey's next question.

"Where's Rudy?"

They all turned to the corral. The corral the horse hadn't left since he was brought there. Rudy was—

"Gone," Beck said, racing to the open gate, his heart pounding through his chest. "Oh, God. He and Dani are both gone."

"You don't think— " Aubrey's hand clutched her throat.

"I don't know what to think," he said, searching in all directions.

"Let's try to put some answers together," Laura said. "Cassidy, you're the last one to see Dani, right?"

Cassidy grabbed Beck, tears filling her eyes as she balanced on her toes. "I'm so sorry. I shouldn't have let her go by herself. This is my fault. I should have stayed with her."

He steadied her, working hard to keep his voice calm. "It's not anyone's fault, Cassidy. We just need to find her. That's our focus."

"Exactly," Laura said. "First, let's check and see if anyone saw her."

A clipped nod was all Beck managed. His entire life hung in the balance until his niece was found. "Cassidy, check with your Dad and at his place. Dani used to go there with you sometimes."

Cassidy nodded and took off at a run.

"I'll check with the ranch hands. Aubrey, you and Laura check around the house. You know a few of Dani's haunts by now."

"Will do." They headed for the back of the house. Beck turned toward the arena where his men were installing upgraded rails.

Fifteen minutes later, everyone at Hope Ranch stood in the parking area, scratching heads full of worry.

"She's taken Rudy and run away," Beck said. "It's the

only explanation." He turned to Aubrey. "Could she have heard anything about George Arenow's plan to take the horse back?"

"What?" Cassidy asked. Several of the hands echoed her question.

"There's no time to explain now. Aubrey, any chance she overheard us talking?"

"I don't know. I was pretty distracted. I wasn't with her when Arenow showed up."

"She was with me all morning," Cassidy cut in. "We were never out front. I never saw the guy myself."

"Was she in the house at all after lunch?"

Cassidy nodded. "I had to check our food stores to place an order. I brought her with me, used it as part of her lessons. She used the bathroom while we were here."

"The bathroom is right next to your office, Beck."

Things looked grim. Beck took a deep breath, trying to calm nerves that would not be calmed. "She must have overheard us and has run off with Rudy so he couldn't be taken. Oh, God, that little girl on that angry horse. I let this happen."

Aubrey touched his cheek. "You said it yourself earlier. This is no one's fault."

"We need to find her." He turned to Amos. "Get horses saddled. We'll form search parties and head to the outer fencing like the spokes on a wheel, and then clockwise along it."

Amos headed for the barn with more speed than Beck had ever seen from him, the other men right behind him.

"I'll change," Aubrey said.

"I need you here."

"You need all the help you can get out on the trail."

"Cassidy and I can stay here and keep looking, if you're good with that," Laura said. "How can I get a hold of you out on the range, in case Dani returns?"

"We've got walkies for ranch work. I'll grab some. Meet back here in five."

He and Aubrey raced for the house where she headed upstairs for riding clothes. Beck grabbed the walkies from the hall closet.

Beck returned to Laura first. They stood there, waiting for Aubrey together.

"I'll go ahead to the barn," Beck said. He couldn't stand still. Action was the only thing that would find Dani, and he needed action to calm his racing nerves.

"The horses aren't ready yet. I can see that from here. Aubrey will be here in a moment, I'm sure. You two ... "

"You two what?" Beck watched the men bringing horses out two by two. She was right. They weren't ready yet. His horse and Aubrey's hadn't been saddled.

"You two seem like you're getting along."

He refocused on Laura. "I'm not having this conversation with you. Not right now, at any rate, while Dani's missing. There are limits to our relationship."

Laura held up her hands. "You're right. There are limits. I only mentioned it because I think it's a good thing. For Dani, especially. Aubrey asked about custody of Dani. Did you know that?"

The worry in Beck's head switched gears. "She wanted Dani?"

"Who wouldn't? She's a great child."

"Aubrey approached you about custody of Dani?"

"She mentioned it, which is why I think— "

Beck barely heard her, so much noise filled his mind, his ears, his heart. Aubrey wanted to take Dani from him? Is that why she'd come? Had she gotten under his skin for a purpose? Maybe everything between them had been a ruse. How had he not seen it?

Beck leaned into Laura's personal space. "I want to make something perfectly clear. No one. Not you, not her, no one will take Dani away from me. I love that child more than life itself and I will fight anyone who tries to remove her from my side."

He didn't notice the look of alarm on Laura's face. "That's not what I meant, Beck. Oh, Lord. I've made things worse. So much worse. I'm sorry. You must understand—"

"I understand perfectly." Beck froze as Aubrey walked out the front door. "This conversation is over." He raced to the barn, not caring if Aubrey followed.

No way in hell she would steal Dani from him. No. Way. In. Hell.

~~~

"Beck," Aubrey called as she raced after him.

He didn't acknowledge her or even turn around. Aubrey understood that kind of focus. Fear for Dani consumed her more than anything had in her life, the same as those months she'd watched Hope slip away.

Beck barked orders, picking directions for everyone. He sounded angry. "Amos, you take Aubrey with you. I'll head off to the north."

"No. I'm going with you," she said to Beck, confused.

His lips were a grim line as he shook his head.

"You can tell me to go with Amos, but I'll still follow you. You shouldn't be out there alone."

He turned on her, pure fury radiating from his gaze. Aubrey stepped back in surprise. What was going on?

"I agree with her," Amos said. "No one should search alone, and I need to go with the newest hands. These walkies aren't that reliable and you might need a rider to race back here."

Beck's inhale held little patience, but he gave a curt
~~~

nod. "Mount up. Let's find my girl." He swung into his saddle and lit out, leaving Aubrey to follow on her own.

Amos helped her into the saddle.

"What's wrong with him?" she asked.

He watched Beck ride off. "I'm not sure. Something's ticked him off. Stay with him. Don't let him do something stupid."

Cassie handed her a bag. "Some food to get you through. Not much, but it'll tide you over if you have to stay out." She waited until Aubrey focused on her. "Get Beck talking. There's some misunderstanding, but I don't know what."

Aubrey stowed the bag and urged Sadie into a gallop to catch up with Beck. It took a while. He'd set a hard pace and had a decent lead. "Beck, slow down. Neither of the horses can keep up this pace long term."

"War Horse can."

"Well, Sadie can't."

"Then go back. I can search just fine by myself. In fact, I prefer it."

His words hit her like a punch in the gut. When he looked at her, dark anger filled his eyes.

Aubrey tried again. "Slow down, Beck. We're far enough out that we need to be paying better attention to what's around us. And apparently, we need to talk."

"I'm done talking to you."

Something she said must have sunk in, because Beck slowed down enough for Aubrey to pace him. They rode in stoic silence, except for occasional calls for Dani and some for Rudy, hoping he'd respond if she wouldn't. At least the silence meant they'd hear if Dani called out to them.

With no clue why Beck's mood had turned so foul, Aubrey went over the events of the last few hours, trying to figure out what she'd done. He'd seemed fine, with her at least, until a few minutes ago. What had changed? Her heart ached to turn back the clock, to stop Dani from running, and to figure out why Beck had somehow switched from loving to hating her.

It hurt. So bad. Her heart was breaking in two, again, and Aubrey didn't have the first idea how to deal with another loss. Hope's death had devastated her. She'd shut down. If Beck turned her away, if he forced her to leave Hope Ranch, and Dani, and him ... She was afraid she wouldn't recover this time.

Aubrey hunched over in her saddle, the pain in her stomach a real-life response to the emotional upheaval.

Beck glanced at her, then gazed forward again, never once asking what was wrong. She loved him and had thought he might be falling for her. Somehow, that had changed but now wasn't the time to skewer herself on that pain-stick. She had to focus on the search for Dani. Aubrey straightened, went back to scanning the landscape and calling Dani's name.

They rode for hours. Day had given way to dusk and dark would settle soon.

"Dani!" Aubrey called, her voice hoarse. She and Beck had settled into calling out at about five-minute intervals, never hearing anything back in response. Glancing in the pack Cassidy had given her, Aubrey pulled out bottled water. She handed one to Beck who took it without a word or nod. She also handed him a sandwich. They chewed in silence, both focused on what little they could see.

"We'll need to stop soon because of the darkness, right?"

"I can ride at night."

"And see behind every tree and bush? If Dani and Rudy remain silent, you could pass right by them and never realize it. Besides, the horses need to rest."

Silence answered her.

"Beck, everyone else has radioed in that they are camping for the night and will pick up the search in the morning."

Again, no answer. Aubrey had about had it with Beck's silent treatment. She stopped Sadie. Off in the distance, she saw a copse of trees. "You might be able to keep this up, but I can't. Keep going if you want. I'll camp for the night to give Sadie some food and water and rest. I have no idea what I did that pissed you off, but driving this hard isn't good for any of us, Dani included."

She turned Sadie toward the trees, not bothering to look back to see what Beck did. Until he wanted to talk, she was done with him. When she reached the trees, she slipped off Sadie's back and stretched, glad to be on terra firma. She tied Sadie off with enough lead to reach the ground, removed her saddle and packs, gave her grain, then poured water from the skin Cassie had given her into a water bag for the horse.

With no tent, she'd need to make do with a fire and her bedroll. Except she'd never once started a fire. Rummaging through the packs she'd pulled off Sadie's back, she gave thanks to whoever thought to put an emergency kit with a flint inside.

She cleared a spot for the fire and pulled together some sticks and materials she thought might burn. At the first strike of the flint, she heard Beck approach and dismount. He took the flint out of her hands and quickly started their fire. Without a single word.

"Gee, thanks," Aubrey said, grabbing her bedroll so she wouldn't have to be anywhere near him. She set it on the opposite side of the fire, then sat down and stared at the flickering flames. Even anger couldn't keep her worry at bay. Where had Dani and Rudy gone? The girl was out here alone. Well, not alone. Rudy would protect Dani as best he could. But he couldn't keep her warm enough. And they'd have no light. She'd be in the dark and scared. Tears wet Aubrey's cheeks. She looked up, past the light of the fire, to the clear night sky dotted with a myriad of stars. "Please be safe, Dani. Please, please, God, keep her safe."

Beck stared at her from his own bedroll, his frown still deep.

"You ready to tell me what happened that you can't look at me without scowling."

Mute again.

"Fine. Goodnight."

Aubrey turned her back to him and laid down, using a pack for a pillow. Totally unsatisfactory, because at the moment, she needed a nice soft pillow to punch. She closed her eyes tight, willing herself to sleep and feeling the weariness in her body. Sleep eluded her, though, replaced by an ache nothing would ease. She had no idea how long she lay there listening to the sounds around them. One sound stood out, a small whine, like some creature searching for a safe place for the night.

"I won't let you take her."

"What?"

"Dani. She's my daughter. You can't have her."

The whine grew stronger. What was it? Distracted, Aubrey didn't answer Beck at first, instead focused on the sound.

"What do you mean, Beck?"

"That social worker told me your plan. That you want custody of Dani."

Two thoughts invaded Aubrey's mind. First, guilt that Beck found out she'd mentioned something to Laura. She'd forgotten all about that. More urgently, the sound she'd heard was getting closer and seemed ... human. Crying?

Aubrey leaped up. "Dani?" she cried, saying her name over and over again.

Beck must have clued into the noise because he raced out of camp with a hasty "stay here" tossed in Aubrey's direction. Moments later, he returned with Dani hugged tightly in his arms, the horse following behind.

"Get Rudy."

She did, her hands shaking so bad it took her three tries to get the reins around the tree branch.

Beck sat by the fire with Dani, hugging her so tight Aubrey couldn't get a look at her. She could see Beck's face though. Tears formed trails through the dirt as he held her. It killed Aubrey to wait, but this was his right. Now that Dani was safe, Beck needed his own fears to settle. Aubrey lifted the walkie from Beck's saddle and walked into the woods, informing everyone that Dani had been found and was okay. They'd camp, then head back in the morning. Afterward, she grabbed the bag with the food in it and sat beside Beck and Dani, willing to wait her turn.

CHAPTER SEVENTEEN

"Where have you been, sweetie? Why did you go? God, never do that again." Beck's voice shook as he spoke. They'd found Dani. And he couldn't stop touching her. While they were searching he'd prayed. Hell, he'd promised to turn over his soul. Long hours of begging for mercy. *Take me. Please. Not her.*

Beck hugged her tight to his chest, to his heart.

A voice, beside him. What was she saying?

"She's all right, Beck. She's all right."

Over and over again, the words infiltrated his mind until they became a cadence that relaxed his breathing and his hold on Dani. Finally, he loosened his arms enough to get a look at her. With her matted hair and tear-streaked face, she looked like a wild pixie.

"Are you hurt anywhere?"

Dani shook her head, her tears subsiding. She reached for Aubrey, and though Beck found it hard to let her go, he did. No matter the issues between them, Aubrey loved Dani.

She mouthed a thank you to Beck as she hugged Dani just as tightly. Dani clung to her, too.

"I'll check on Rudy." He wasn't sure either heard him, but he needed to walk off the adrenaline and emotion. To let it all go now that Dani was safe. When he returned, Dani was eating. Beck smiled. Cassidy thought of everything, including Dani's favorite peanut butter and jelly sandwich.

"Rudy's got food and water."

"And I let everyone know by walkie that we found Dani and she's okay."

Beck nodded. He'd heard her doing that earlier. He took Dani back onto his lap, feeling a sense of peace come over him. Somewhere in the past few months, Dani had become his own child. The last piece of Hope that he'd been afraid he'd lost. Now that he had her back, nothing else mattered. He glanced at Aubrey, who handed Dani some water to drink. Well, almost nothing else.

"To set the record straight, Beck," Aubrey said as she fussed over Dani. "I searched for Dani for weeks after her mother passed. I grew to love her through my time with them. I wanted to raise her myself, to see what kind of woman she would become, and to make certain she always knew how much Hope loved her. When I found her, here, with you— " Tears filled Aubrey's eyes as she looked at Beck. "During my first twenty-four hours here, I might have found Dani, but I also met an ogre who yanked me away from horses and flattened my tires. So yes, in that same time frame, I met and mentioned to Laura that if things didn't work out for Dani here with you, I wanted very much to become her adoptive mother."

She reached in the bag, pulling out wet wipes. "I'm

sorry. I shouldn't have done that. I hadn't gotten to know you, and I didn't understand how good you were for Dani or how much you loved her. How much she loved you. I know now. I'm so sorry that you were hurt by what I said to Laura. I only ever wanted to be part of Dani's life." Her voice caught. "Neither of us knew the other well then. I'd hoped you'd learned enough about me by now to know I would never try to separate you two."

Just like that, the final cog fell into place in Beck's life. He got it. All the misunderstanding, remorse, and worry fell away, making room for better emotions to fill the empty spaces. For love.

"I know that now. I'm sorry. I tried and convicted you without giving you a chance to explain." Beck leaned over Dani to reach for Aubrey, showing her through his kiss how sorry he was, how much she meant to him. "I love you, Aubrey. I wasn't looking for it. Hell, I didn't have room for it in among all the guilt. You've opened my heart to new possibilities. You and Rudy and Dani and Hope." He held out his arm, inviting her closer.

Aubrey tucked herself into his side. "I wasn't looking for anything either, except a way out of my grief, yet I found you. I can't imagine a life without you, Beck. Without Dani. I love you both so much."

He kissed her again, imbuing his touch with all the promise their a future together.

Dani squirmed out of his arms as they broke the kiss. She touched Beck's cheek. "Daddy," she croaked, also reaching for Aubrey's cheek. "Aubrey."

Aubrey's mouth went slack, and Beck's jaw hit the dirt. Dani had called him Daddy. His heart overflowed as the last huge ball of worry disappeared.

"You're talking, Dani. You spoke!" Aubrey said.

Dani nodded, a shy smile on her face.

Beck hugged her, his eyes misty. The first time Dani had called him Daddy. Aubrey was crying, too.

"Why didn't you speak before this?" Aubrey asked.

"I listened."

"For what?"

"For Mommy."

Beck wiped the tears from Dani's face. "Why, sweetie?"

"Mommy said if I listened really hard, I'd hear her whispering in the wind."

Beck swallowed the huge lump in his throat as understanding dawned. All this time, trying to figure out why his niece was mute, and it had been this simple.

"I know you miss your mother. We all do. So very much. I like to go out at night, look up at the stars, and talk to your mother. That's what you do, isn't it?"

"She doesn't answer me."

"Not in the way you want her to, but she does answer. She brought Aubrey to us, didn't she?"

Dani nodded, clutching Aubrey's hand.

"And she brought Rudy to us."

Dani smiled. "I like Rudy."

"You should. I didn't want to tell you before this, but Rudy was your mother's horse."

Dani and Aubrey stared at him.

"You might not remember, Dani, but your mother owned Rudy. She boarded him at a stable near your house."

Dani scrunched up her face. "I 'member horse."

"That was Rudy. When she got sick, she couldn't take care of him any longer and sold him." Beck looked at Aubrey. "Hope's attorney mentioned that she'd sold Rudy to a reputable stable. When Rudy was rescued, the people who saved him searched for the prior owner. Since I was executor, they reached out to me. So," he said, tapping

Dani on the nose, "that explains why you kept sneaking outside to see Rudy at night."

Dani hid her face in Beck's chest. His love for her gushed over.

"It's all right. I kept watch over you while you were with Rudy. That's my job. To keep you safe."

He pulled Aubrey back to his side. "To keep both of you safe."

Aubrey gazed up at Beck, the love showing in her eyes. "Just as we're here to keep you safe. Right, Dani?"

"Right!"

He squinted at them both. "And there will be no more going out at night alone?"

His question was met with silence.

"But, like I mentioned before, Dani, maybe we can go outside together before bedtime and say goodnight to Rudy, and to Mommy."

Dani nodded her head emphatically. They sat there, a new family, staring at the fire. Soon Dani's head lolled.

"She's asleep," Beck said.

"She must be exhausted. I'll lay out a bedroll."

"Lay them both out. Together. We'll put Dani between us."

Aubrey's smile was all the answer he needed.

~~~

The next morning, they got on the trail early. Dani rode in front of Beck while Aubrey rode Sadie and led Rudy by a lead rope attached to his halter. By lunch, they'd come within sight of the ranch house. Everyone rode out to meet them. Even Cassidy, who, despite her fear of horses, sat behind her father looking like a ghost had taken over her body.

Aubrey laughed along with everyone else. Today was a happy day. They'd found Dani safe and sound, and a new
~~~

promise had sprouted between herself and Beck. One she hoped would take a lifetime to keep. She watched him, laughing at the antics of the riders who raced around them stirring up dust, her heart so full she thought it might burst.

Thank you, Hope, for showing me the way back to happiness. Thank you, Mara, for bringing us together.

Beck reached out his hand for hers, which she gladly accepted once Amos took Rudy's lead from her. Aubrey didn't hesitate to show everyone around them that she and Beck were a couple.

They were a rowdy bunch as they rode into the area between the barn and the ranch house. Laura waited for them there, the same wide grin on her face. Beck handed Dani down to her, jumped from War Horse's back, and came around to help Aubrey dismount. He held her for a long moment, kissing her with a promise that said she would not be sleeping alone tonight, or any night henceforth.

"I'm hungry," Dani said, stealing the show as man, woman, and mount all went silent and gaped at the no longer silent child.

"It's a long story," Beck said to the group, who whooped and hollered some more. Cassie picked Dani up to hug her, handing her off to Amos. One by one, everyone got their chance to hold and hug.

Just as the celebratory crowd headed for the house, Amos nodded toward the road. "Company."

A truck pulling a horse trailer closed in on them, stopping in front of Rudy's corral. A Sheriff's SUV came in behind. Had the sheriff come to uphold Arenow's legal right to Rudy? Aubrey found his lead rope and clutched it tight as Dani moved beside her and hugged her leg.

Arenow got out of his truck and slammed the door. "I'm here for my horse," he said.

"Rudy will never be your horse."

Aubrey almost smiled as all the ranch hands crowded in behind Beck.

Arenow took a step back. "You can't do anything to stop me, Hawthorne. I've got the legal right."

"Not anymore, you don't," Sheriff Charles said from behind Arenow. A man and woman stood with him.

"This here says I do." Arenow waved the papers he held. "It's your job to uphold the law."

"There's a stronger law that I uphold. That of God's kind will for all his creatures, humans and horses alike. We have proof of your abusive treatment of the equines in your possession." The woman handed the sheriff a file, which he gave to Arenow. "These are a few pages from a journal, made by a man in your employ several years ago, that give examples of how you treat horses. It's been turned over to the District Attorney in your county, the breeders' association, and the local humane society. I believe they served papers on your ranch this morning and are searching it now for additional proof while we stand here chatting. By the time they're done, you won't own a dog. Your horse-breeding days are over. And— " Charles reached behind him for another set of papers. "This is an official court stay, allowing the horse in question to remain here pending legal efforts to transfer him permanently to Hope Ranch."

Arenow, now red in the face, glared at the sheriff. "You can't do this. You can't go on my property without me being there."

"Legally, we can. You have a manager who you authorized to act in your absence. Funny, but I heard from the authorities there that he had a big grin on his face as he waved them in."

"You're done, Arenow," Beck said. He took a step toward him. The entirety of Hope Ranch stepped forward with him. "Get off my property."

After opening and closing his mouth a few times, Arenow finally managed to speak. "This isn't over, Hawthorne."

"Yes. It is. If you ever step foot on my ranch again, I'll have you thrown in jail for trespassing."

Arenow strode to his truck and peeled out, leaving a dust storm in his wake.

Beck shook the sheriff's hand. "Thanks, Pat. I owe you one."

"You don't owe me anything. Been hearing things about that guy. I don't countenance animals being mistreated. I think he might actually do some jail time this go-round. Finally. Feels good to be part of taking him down." He nodded toward Dani, who still hugged Aubrey's leg. "That the little girl you were searching for?"

Beck nodded, motioning for Aubrey and Dani to join him. He swung Dani up in his arms.

"Well, then, I guess everything's turned out fine."

"Care to join us for some lunch?" Beck included the people with the sheriff in his glance.

"Some other time. We've got to get these papers filed. Didn't have a chance before coming out here."

Beck grinned. "No matter what you say, I owe you. Stop out anytime."

"I'll do that," he said, tipping his hat to the ladies.

After the sheriff left, Aubrey once again handed Rudy's lead rope to Amos. He took it carefully, eyeing the horse. Rudy turned his head toward Amos and huffed, bringing his head up. When Amos took a quick step back, everyone laughed.

"I don't think he'll be any more trouble," Beck said. "Rudy's heart has come home."

"Rudy stays here?" Dani asked.

"You bet he does," Beck said. He took Aubrey's hand, then led the menagerie that had become Aubrey's new family into the ranch house.

"We'll get the horses settled and join you," Amos said.

"Thank you. This little one needs cleaning up," Beck said.

"I'll start lunch," Cassie chimed in.

"See you all in a while." There would be no working today, other than bare necessities. This was a day for celebration.

Laura stopped them at the house. "Now that things are settled and our girl is safe, I'll head home. I— "

Aubrey knew, from her own social work, what bothered Laura. "It all worked out."

"I'm sorry," she blurted. "Beck, I should have never mentioned my conversation with Aubrey. She'd just arrived, and I was eager to hear more about Dani's life before."

"You helped us figure out that we both wanted the same thing," Beck said. He smiled at Dani and Aubrey. "Turned out pretty well, so I thank you."

Laura nodded, reaching up to smooth Dani's hair. "It was always apparent that you both love this child very much. Dani, now maybe we can have some of those conversations I've been wanting to have."

Dani was almost asleep on Beck's shoulder.

"Looks like you'd better get her cleaned up before she drops off. I'll check in on you in a few days." Laura stepped off the porch but turned back to them. "Oh, and I'm recommending adoption. Dani's obviously in the best place possible. Should I be listing one name or two on the papers?"

"Two." Beck and Aubrey spoke at the same time, except it didn't feel like a jinx. More like the promise of a fresh new start for all of them.

Laura laughed. "I'm good with that." She waved and headed to her car.

Aubrey and Beck watched her leave.

"What say we get this girl cleaned up," Aubrey said.

"It might be too late already."

Dani was sound asleep on Beck's shoulder.

"Maybe a nap is more important?"

"Agreed."

After spreading a sheet to keep her bed clean, they laid Dani on it and covered her up. Aubrey moved into Beck's embrace as they watched the peaceful rise and fall of Dani's chest.

"I think she'll finally be happy. She's come to terms with her mother being gone," Beck said.

"I will always miss Hope, so vibrant, so full of life. Right up until the end." Finally, the mention of Hope didn't bring tears to her eyes. The ache still filled a corner of Aubrey's heart, but she could move forward and be happy now. Hope would want that. She hugged Beck tight.

"I had a long conversation with Hope before Dani disappeared. I still have a lot to atone for," Beck said, "but thanks to you and this little angel, I'm no longer crushed by remorse that made it impossible to breathe, much less live." He kissed the top of Aubrey's head.

"I love her so much, Beck."

"I do, too." Beck turned Aubrey to face him. "As much as I love you."

Aubrey sighed. "I feel like I've come home."

"I know you have."

EPILOGUE

"You need to be quiet until I ask, all right?" Beck had his doubts Dani would listen. "Can you do that?" It had become almost impossible to quiet the imp now that she was speaking again.

"I can. I can." Dani fairly bubbled with excitement, bouncing around his office like a Slinky on steroids.

Beck handed her the small box. "Don't lose this. I'll tell you when to let her see it."

Dani nodded and nodded and nodded, making Beck laugh. A good thing, too. Even though he had a good idea of the outcome, he was unusually nervous.

"No time like the present," he said, standing. He tucked an already tucked shirt into his jeans and ran a hand over hair that hadn't seen a hat yet today. Holding his hand out to Dani, he waited until she stowed the box in her pocket, then settled her small hand in his. He loved how her little fingers fit in his big palm. He loved everything about his daughter. The adoption papers were in process and it wouldn't be long until Dani was legally his. His and Aubrey's. Now it was time to make their family complete. "Let's go find Aubrey."

Aubrey sat at the kitchen table with Mara, who'd arrived two days earlier to see for herself how things had worked out. Based on Beck's conversations with her, things had happened exactly as she'd planned. He didn't like busybodies, but in this case, he'd thanked Mara privately for sending Aubrey to him.

Now, it was time to finish this thing. Aubrey looked up at Beck with such deep, shining love, she took his breath away. He wasn't sure he deserved her, but he planned to spend the rest of his life trying to be the man who did. Beck took a deep breath. Before he could go down on a knee, Dani thrust the box in Aubrey's surprised face.

"We want to marry you. We want you to be my mommy," she shouted, hugging Aubrey tight.

"Thanks, sweetie," Beck said, prying the box from Dani's small hands. "Mind if I take over?"

Dani let go of the box and raced around the table onto Mara's lap, elbows on table and chin in hands to watch.

Beck knelt on one knee in front of Aubrey. "Now that the secret's out ... " He took a deep breath. "Aubrey, when you arrived, I didn't want you here."

She chuckled. "I didn't exactly want to be here."

"I'm glad I flattened your tires. If I hadn't, you might have left, and I'd never have known the love I feel for you. Every morning, I open my eyes and I'm in awe that you're with me. You make the sun shine brighter, you give life meaning. And you give me ... everything. I want to do that for you."

"You already do." She touched his cheek. "You've given me all I've ever wanted, including Dani."

"I want to do that forever. To have you here, with me, and be a family with our daughter. Aubrey Gannet, will you be Dani's mother in all ways? Will you marry me and be my wife?"

"I already have in my heart," she whispered.

He grinned and kissed her, relief pouring out of him as the last chink in his armor broke and dissipated. God, he loved her.

Beck opened the box.

~~~

Aubrey gasped. She hadn't thought she could be any more surprised until she saw the ring.

"It was my mother's," Beck said.

"I know." Aubrey's voice was a whisper. She reached out to the box, then pulled her hand back in awe. "I remember this ring."

"I thought it was lost. Sorting through all of Hope's boxes, I found it."

"She wore it all the time."

"She never married, as you know, but she loved this ring."

"Oh, Beck, I'm not sure … "

"If you don't like it, we can find something else. But I think Hope would like you to wear it. She'd like the idea of us together."

"I agree." She held out a shaky hand as Beck took the ring from the box and held it up.

"What do you say? Want to do this?"

"Oh, yes," she breathed. "I want to very much. So yes, Beck. I'll gladly marry you."

"Thank God."

He placed the ring on her finger, though Aubrey only had eyes for him at the moment. Beck pulled her up and into his arms. "I love you, future Mrs. Hawthorne."
~~~

"I love you right back." Aubrey poured her heart into the kiss that cemented their future. Beck Hawthorne was her soul-mate, her savior, and the man she wanted to be with for always.

"Yippee!" Dani leaped off Mara's lap and bowled into them. Beck bent down and picked her up for a three-way hug. "Now I have a Daddy and two Mommies!"

"Yes, kiddo, you do." Aubrey would make sure Dani always remembered how loved she was by both her mothers.

"I knew you two would be perfect for each other. Congratulations," Mara said.

"Thanks," Aubrey said. "Thank you for making it happen."

"But," Beck said with mock sternness, "no more meddling. We've got it from here."

Mara raised her hands, laughing. "Deal!"

Beck looked at Dani. "What say we go give Rudy the news?"

Aubrey loved that idea. So did Dani, who squirmed to get out of his arms.

Beck set her down and she raced ahead of them. Taking Aubrey's hand in his, they followed.

Rudy waited for them at the edge of the corral. It still surprised Aubrey how quickly the horse had tamed. He'd just needed Hope's people around him so he could let go of his past and embrace his new family. Now, all the lost souls of Hope Ranch had let go of their pain and found the joy in life again.

"We're getting married, Rudy," Dani said, climbing up the rail to hug the horse.

Rudy nickered, leaning his head into Dani, then reaching toward Aubrey's outstretched hand.

"We're a family now, boy. And you're part of that

family. Somehow, you realize that, don't you?"

Rudy nudged her hand, almost as if nodding.

Beck, standing behind Aubrey, encircled her waist with his arms. "I think Rudy's heart kept us together while we figured out our own."

Aubrey leaned back against him. "He saved us."

"And you saved me," Beck said, turning her in his arms.

She'd never tire of his kisses. Each one seemed like the first and filled her with hope and love and need. "Thank you for flattening my tires, Beck Hawthorne."

"Any time," he said, grinning.

"Oh!" Aubrey started when she realized Rudy had found the carrot she always kept in her back pocket. He happily munched while Dani, Beck, and Aubrey laughed. Even Rudy, when he finished eating, looked like he had a smile on his face.

They stood there quietly, enjoying each other. For the moment, the circle of life had completed itself and the future looked bright. Aubrey glanced up at the clear blue sky. *Thank you, Hope. For letting me know you, for guiding me through my grief and into the arms of your brother.*

Happier than ever before, Aubrey watched Dani scrub at Rudy's neck. There was no halfway with this child. She gave one hundred and fifty percent to everything she tried. Just like her father, Aubrey's soon-to-be husband.

"I don't want to wait," Aubrey said.

"Hmm?" Beck distracted himself by kissing her neck, which sent needy chills down her back.

"I said, I don't want to wait. I don't want a big wedding. I just want you. And Dani."

"Isn't the guy supposed to be the one to say that?"

Aubrey shrugged. "It's how I feel."

"Me, too. How about we go sign up for that wedding

license tomorrow?"

"Maybe Amos can marry us? It's Montana. I've heard you don't need a license to officiate. You just need the marriage license."

Beck hugged her tight. "I like that. Saturday?"

"Five days from now? That sounds absolutely perfect. And right here, with Rudy. This is where we started."

Beck nodded. "And this is where we'll begin the next chapter in our lives."

He kissed her again, a long, full-of-promise touch that flooded Aubrey's heart with love. They stood there, man, woman, child, and horse. Ready for the future.

Together.

At peace.

Loved.

The End.

Thank you for reading **Rudy's Heart.** If you enjoyed this book, please consider leaving a review wherever you prefer, and know that it would be greatly appreciated.

For new release information and news about Laurie Ryan, please join her newsletter. More information is available on her website at **www.laurieryanauthor.com**.

AUTHOR'S NOTE

How many stories are born from dreams? They say a writer's best tools are a notepad & pen beside their bed. Most of my stories start with a real life picture or incident. Not Rudy. He wanted to be in a book so bad, he came to me in sleep. I don't remember the specifics, only that Rudy, a paint, came to the rescue.

I don't claim to know horses well. In fact, I'm a city girl with a country love—horses. All my life, I've considered them special beings. I swore, when I was ten years old, I'd own my own horse eventually. Somehow, that dream went by the wayside as I wandered through my life. But my love for these majestic animals never waned.

The themes of my stories center around the idea that doing things alone is never as successful as with help. Rudy's Heart does not deviate from that theme, and neither did I. A special thank you to Kathleen, whose love and respect of these special animals helped me remember that ten-year-old girl who wanted nothing more than to be around horses. Kathleen answered all my horse questions and helped me to understand Rudy so much better. Any errors in horse behavior, tack, or other equine things are mine alone.

As well, many thanks to my CP's, Lavada Dee and Faye Avalon, to Marie Tuhart, who makes certain I keep writing, to Dar Albert for a cover that made me cry, and to Libby Doyle for her amazing editing.

Last, but not least, thank you, readers. You make it all worthwhile!
Laurie Ryan

BOOKLIST

Contemporary romance stories by Laurie Ryan
Tropical Persuasions Series
Stolen Treasures
Pirate's Promise
Dare To Love

Standalone
Northern Lights
Healing Love
(also part of the Holiday Magic anthology)
Lost and Found

Women's Fiction by Laurie Ryan
Show Me

Fantasy by Laurie Ryan
Survival
Enlightenment
Birthright

ABOUT THE AUTHOR

Laurie Ryan writes contemporary romance and fantasy. Growing up a devoted reader, Laurie Ryan immersed herself in the diverse works of authors like Tolkien and Woodiwiss. She is passionate about every aspect of a book: beginning, middle, and end. She can't arrive to a movie five minutes late, has never been able to read the end of a book before the beginning, and is a strong believer in reading the book before seeing the movie.

Laurie lives in the beautiful Pacific Northwest, in the shadow of Mt. Rainier and a short drive to beach-walking next to the Pacific Ocean, with her handsome, he-can-fix-anything husband.

www.laurieryanauthor.com

A PEEK AT LOST AND FOUND

(a Laurie Ryan novella)

CHAPTER ONE

"Who says you can't go back home?" Sarah mumbled as she walked through Riverhaven, the quaint town where she'd grown up. It had taken eleven years and one very hard lesson, coupled with a lot of soul-searching, to bring her back here. But back she was. She'd arrived late last night with an SUV full of boxes and an agenda. There were a few hurdles to be crossed before she'd know if this had been the right choice.

Good or bad, she was here to stay. At least, that's what the new cards in her purse said, along with her almost empty gas tank.

Passing the town park, Sarah stopped, amazed by what she saw. The ancient tree still stood there, proud and venerable. Maple leaves covered it, some green, some yellowed from summer's heat. She patted bark already warm from the morning sun. Many kisses had been given freely or stolen beneath its limbs and carved initials immortalized countless young loves.

Sarah traced a set encircled by a heart as an old melancholy threaded its way through her. If only someone had carved her initials. She'd longed for a boyfriend back then. Maybe even one in particular, with dark, chestnut hair, a crooked smile, and nerd-glasses.

But that hadn't happened. Not for her. So, with nothing to keep her in Riverhaven, she'd lit out of town right after graduation. Why stay, when the world was chalk full of opportunities just waiting for her?

Turns out, there wasn't enough to keep her in the big city, either. After losing, well, just about everything she owned, Sarah had figured it out. She'd learned the hard way that home wasn't determined by those you thought loved you. Home was in the heart, and Sarah's had led her back to Riverhaven. All the turmoil in her life had been replaced by peacefulness once she'd made the decision to come back, so after years working for a small consulting firm, Sarah had left the steady income, along with her un-savvy boyfriend, and come home to set up her own future.

Needing an income in a hurry, Sarah had kicked off her organizational consulting company, *Find Your Life*, from a distance, ordering cards and advertising in the local paper while still in Seattle. Because of that, she already had a few appointments set up for this, her first week back. Hitting the ground running was important since she'd spent virtually all her money renting a cheap apartment. She had just enough left to buy a few groceries.

Which was why she'd left her SUV, still packed to the gills with all that remained of her life in Seattle, parked outside her new home. No need to use precious gas when this town was so walkable.

This morning had proven that, even as organized as she'd been while packing and loading, the best-laid plans could kick you when you were down. She'd dug through box after box looking for the outfit she wanted to wear to her first appointment, then wondered why her flat iron wasn't in the bathroom box.

By the time she'd left the apartment, she'd needed the calming walk. Her highlighted hair was wavy when it should be straight, her makeup was minimal, limited to what she'd found in her purse, and she wore khakis, not the slacks she preferred. At least she'd found a nice top in a shade of green that complimented her hazel eyes. If a couple errant wrinkles showed, well, she'd pretend they weren't there and hoped the client overlooked them as well.

Leaning against the wide trunk of the tree, Sarah turned her face to the sun's soothing warmth, enjoying it while she could. Riverhaven would bake later as the temperature climbed to a newsworthy record high.

Glancing at her watch, Sarah realized she needed to move. No way did she want to be late. Heading toward the address she'd been given, Sarah enjoyed the nuances of a small town life. Not much stirred yet, and there were no traffic jams, no sirens. Just peace and quiet broken by the hum of an occasional car.

This morning's disastrous start had rattled her a bit, but Sarah regrouped on the walk, confident and ready for her first official *Find Your Life* appointment. She hoped the client, Rick Larson, hired her. She'd need to ramp the business up fast or she'd be living under that tree before long.

Rick Larson. The name, and the address he'd given her, evoked memories she couldn't stop from flooding through her. Memories of the house next door, and the boy who lived inside.

Rounding the corner, nostalgia swarmed around her like the first scent of lavender each summer, bringing a wistful smile to her face. The old neighborhood had changed so little. Large maples still lined the road, keeping it green and shady through summer and bringing the street alive with color in the fall. Some houses were more rundown than she remembered, others showed fresh renovations. New ones occupied a vacant lot where she'd spent her childhood building cardboard cities with the neighborhood kids.

Her parents no longer lived here. They'd sold everything, including the home she'd grown up in, to motor-home around the country. Currently, they were parked somewhere in the Midwest. That kind of rootless existence didn't appeal to Sarah. She preferred the familiarity of living in one place, the predictability of the world around her, and the efficiency of knowing the best places to shop, eat, or whatever.

So why were her nerves aflutter? Sarah stood in front of the address of her first appointment, right next door to the house she'd been raised in, holding her stomach to still the butterflies. Her teen years had been spent staring at this house. Night after night. Hoping *he* might notice her.

Fred Larson.

Even after all this time, her heart pounded. She'd loved him with a forever kind of love, and he'd never acknowledged her presence beyond an occasional glance, or spoken to her beyond a quick "hey" while they waited for the bus. His lack of regard had crushed her.

Now her possible first client seemed to be some sort of relation to the man who'd broken her heart without ever knowing it. Sarah shook herself out of the doldrums and strode to the door, hesitating a moment before knocking to be sure she had her emotions under control.

When the door opened, she swallowed a gasp as Mr. Tall, Dark, and way, way too Handsome stared back at her.

Get a grip, girl. Sarah clenched and unclenched her hands, letting her breath out in a whoosh as a flush that must border on crimson warmed her face. What was the matter with her? She'd seen good-looking guys before, had even flirted with them. This one robbed her of speech. There was something about him. Maybe the broad shoulders, or the fact that he was so tall?

He watched her, his eyes dark with focused intensity, apparently waiting for her to speak first.

Reaching deep for an ounce of professionalism, Sarah tucked an errant piece of hair behind her ear and stuck out her hand. "Hi, I'm from *Find Your Life*." Good. Hardly any stammer. "My name is—"

"Sarah Rose," he finished with a voice so warm and inviting, she wanted to melt into a puddle at his feet. "It's wonderful to see you again."

She'd met him? Sarah would remember meeting a man this good looking. "Umm..."

His smile faltered. "You don't remember me, do you?"

"I remember a Fred Larson." Oh, boy did she remember Fred. Dark, short hair. Shorter than this man's hair that just brushed his collar. Those chocolate eyes seemed so familiar. Was he a relative?

"I go by Rick now."

Sarah's mouth dropped, her heart hammering in her chest as she peered more closely at him. This was Fred? *Her* Fred? Well, in her mind, he'd always been hers. "Fred? I mean, Rick? I—I didn't recognize you. You've changed so much. And the name threw me, I guess."

"I can understand the confusion. I dropped the Fred in Fredrick when I headed to college. Figured I might fit in better."

"How'd that go?"

His smile returned. "Not well until I replaced the nerdy glasses with contacts." He shrugged. "Did better after that."

Better? Sarah rubbed at a spot on her chest. Had the temperature just jumped a few degrees?

"You, on the other hand, haven't changed at all," he said, motioning for her to enter.

The crimson that had receded from her face returned full force. Sara ducked her head, unsure if that was a compliment, yet wanting it to be.

"So," she said, trying for some equilibrium. "You live in your childhood home?"

Rick left the door open and showed her to the living room. Dank, humid, air made it seem warmer than outside. A quick glance around showed older, frayed furniture and dust. A lot of dust.

"No, I don't live here. I live in the city."

"Seattle?" Had they been in the same city this whole time?

He shook his head. "Portland. A bit of a drive from here. My father passed away two months ago," Rick continued.

"I'm so sorry," Sarah said. She hadn't heard.

He waved a hand. "Thank you, but different life-goals had estranged us until recently."

She'd heard the oil-and-water fights back then, loud enough to cause the neighbors to close their windows. His father wanted a football star for a son and ended up with a computer geek.

"He didn't suffer," Rick said. "I'm grateful for that."

"Your mom is gone too, I heard."

"Right after graduation." He looked around, his voice tinged with sadness. "There's only me now."

Sarah almost reached out to him, offering solace. He'd been an only child, and it saddened her to think he was alone in the world. She glanced at his left hand. No ring.

"I hope you've got someone who helps you. A wife or girlfriend, maybe?"

Shaking his head, Rick waved a hand in the air. "No wife, not even the hint of a girlfriend. Tried. But after resettling in the city, I never found anyone I wanted to spend that much time with."

Had his gaze intensified? Sarah fidgeted, unwilling to dig too deep into the satisfaction that his denial of any relationship gave her.

"You?"

The contentment warming her belly lurched and became a sour candy playing Pong in her stomach. She wasn't prepared to discuss her ex. She'd stuck with him longer than he'd stuck with any of his get-rich-quick schemes and she didn't want to dwell on where that had left her. Done with ultra-modern, driven, self-employed businessmen, she'd closed the door on dating anyone even remotely like that ever again.

"Uh, no" she answered. "No one. At least, no one worth mentioning."

"Me, either." His grin returned. "When I saw your ad, I was astounded. You're the answer to my prayers, Sarah Rose."

Sarah almost stumbled as her world stuttered to a halt. Seconds ticked away. *You're the answer to my prayers.* She'd wanted him to say those words back in high school, longed for them so much she'd chosen not to date anyone. She'd gone solo to her senior prom, hoping against hope for one last chance.

Sarah looked up into his face, wishing those words meant what she'd hoped for all those years ago and mentally berating her heart for the reminder.

Focused on tamping down ancient emotions, she almost missed the emotion in Rick's gaze. Raw. Needy. All covered up so fast, she couldn't be sure if she saw it or imagined it.

He cleared his throat, then swallowed. "I, umm, need someone to help me sort through everything here, figure out what's worth selling and what should be trashed."

"Oh." Disappointment hit her so hard, she almost stepped back, barely stopping herself. Of course, he meant the estate. That's why he'd asked her to come. It had nothing to do with their non-relationship from the past. Nothing at all. The house is what he needed help with. Work. Organizing. What she did. That's what he'd prayed for.

The old pain from unrequited memories rushed to her heart, the long-buried yearning cutting her like new wounds. She struggled to find some balance to her emotions, digging deep to put the lid back on that box. Sarah straightened, squaring her shoulders against the old pain.

"That's exactly what I do. Sort and organize," she said, pasting a smile on her face.

Rick nodded, indicating she should sit on the couch, which was thankfully devoid of dust.

"Excellent," he said. "So, have you been back in town long? I drove up a few days ago, but had no clue you were even here until I saw your ad in the local paper."

"My advance attack, so I could hit the town running when I arrived." She glanced at her watch. "A whole twelve hours ago."

The look of confusion on his face almost made her laugh.

"I set up the bones of this business from afar. I've been living in Seattle."

"I thought about starting out there after college. I chose to go south instead. If I may ask, how come you're moving back here?"

"I got...tired of the city. I kicked off the advertising, loaded up my things, and arrived here last night. I haven't even unpacked."

"Oh," he said. "If we need to put this off—"

"Not at all. I'm organized and ready to go." Sarah crossed her fingers behind her back. "I can manage both."

"Perfect. Can you start today? Things are pretty crazy for me right now at work, so the sooner I get this done, the sooner I can put it on the market." He looked around. "I don't even know where to start."

He wanted her to begin today, the exact answer she'd been hoping for. Sarah tamped down her enthusiasm and nodded.

"Perfect." Rick smiled and reached for her hand. "I'm glad it's you."

If he held her hand overlong, only Sarah noticed. It was hard not to with the energy thrumming through their touch, at least for her. Rick Larson looked cool and collected and not one bit affected by their meeting. The complete opposite of her. *He's glad it's me?* She was astonished he even remembered her. Her interpretation pushed flawed meaning into his words. She needed to remember that he hadn't noticed her in high school. He'd only contacted her because of business. Rick Larson wanted her to work for him. That was all.

Sarah had staked her future on being successful with *Find Your Life*, so keeping this all about business was her only option no matter what her heart tried to tell her. As if he'd even consider it being more, anyhow. Rick Larson was good looking in a way she'd never found another to match. He was tall, but not too tall. Dark, but not mysteriously so. When he smiled, everything about him warmed her. He'd always been an introverted bookworm. Now, it looked as though Rick had developed people skills.

Boy, had he developed skills.

Sarah would be hard-pressed to keep her mind on the task at hand, but she had to. She could not screw her life up. Not again.

She opened her portfolio and pulled the pen out of its sleeve. "Where should we start?"

To keep up with Laurie Ryan news, please join her newsletter. More information can be found at **www.laurieryanauthor.com**.